By the same author

Earth Cell
The Accrington Folly
The Earth Party
The Grey Tractor
Life With An Invented Father
The Shadow of Innocence
Tristram Shandy Uncovered

The Footloose Pilgrims

George Marshall

Published by New Generation Publishing in 2017

Copyright © George Marshall 2017

Cover design by Jacqueline Abromeit

First Edition

The author asserts the moral right under the Copyright, Designs and Patents Act 1988 to be identified as the author of this work.

All Rights reserved. No part of this publication may be reproduced, stored in a retrieval system or transmitted, in any form or by any means without the prior consent of the author, nor be otherwise circulated in any form of binding or cover other than that in which it is published and without a similar condition being imposed on the subsequent purchaser.

www.newgeneration-publishing.com

1

Staring at the moving luggage is mesmerising—dizzying. A hypnotic effect not unwelcome in its blurring of the lamenting thoughts turning in his head. He could easily fall onto the carousel, a piece of baggage repeatedly circulating until one day, silky black hair falling over her face, Pauline reaches out to reclaim him. The sight of his bag rouses Morris from this bittersweet fantasy, too late to prevent it from starting out on another circuit.

He studies the people near him, each grimly holding position close to the moving belt. He wonders if any of them are with his group. Damn! Nearly missed it again, making a grab for the grey holdall. Lyon Airport is much like any other, frenetic and with an ambience bearing the accumulated tensions of airborne travellers. Leaving the exit from Arrivals he is confronted by several people holding up signs. He makes for the man who has *Footloose* hand-written in black marker on white card.

'You must be Morris Matthews—everyone else is here. I'm Dave, the trek leader.'

The emphasis this fit-looking man places on 'trek' is not encouraging, a companionable stroll along the old pilgrim route was what he had imagined.

He follows Dave to where a group of over a dozen men and women are waiting, and is at once reassured. Several seem quite old, well beyond fifty, a birthday which, for Morris, already looms like a watershed. A few look overweight. There is some nodding and murmurings of welcome as he joins them. His eyes are drawn to two women in close conversation. It is the golden blondness of one of them that attracts his attention. Since Pauline he has avoided looking at women with black hair, enough regrets without the addition of this sensual trigger of hurtful memories. He has developed a conviction that he will only salve the emotional rawness by an amorous involvement with a woman of opposite beauty. He glances at his watch—what would she be doing now? God! He has to stop this.

Morris troops off with the others behind Dave who leads them onto the coach for the journey to Le Puy.

'Jerry Vroobel,' says the man who takes the seat next to Morris.

'Vroobel?' Morris uncertain if he had heard rightly.

'Yes—a Jewish name.'

Morris, introduces himself to this younger man, who without further formality asks what made him chose this particular holiday.

To find a Golden Goddess who will rid me of the spell cast by the Black One, says his mind.

'I think the idea came from reading *The Canterbury Tales*,' his voice declares.

'There I would have been the Sergeant of the Law—has a better ring to it than solicitor.'

'You know Chaucer?'

'At university—Middle English was part of the degree.'

'I did a WEA course last year, thought Chaucer's fourteenth century England would make a welcome change from worrying about the state of the country in the twenty-first,' says Morris.

'*Whan that April with his showres soote. The drought of March has perce to the roote, and bathed every vein in swich licour,*' says Jerry. 'I used to be able to quote whole chunks of the Prologue.'

'Which of the characters best translates into social worker?' Morris asks.

'One of the nuns, I reckon,' smiles Jerry.

During the journey Morris learns that Jerry works for a legal practice in Manchester, specialising in corporate law. 'No court scenes full of human drama in my job,' he says.

'I don't even have a job at present,' Morris tells his new acquaintance. He wonders why Jerry is holidaying alone; is he too trying to forget a woman?

At the hotel Morris notes that the blond-haired woman

and her brunette companion are allocated a double room. He is given a single room. He tries the bed, stretching out, waiting until it is time go down for dinner. Alone in the silence and stillness, a leaden emptiness lies within him, the white pillow a cheerless comfort without the spread of Pauline's raven hair. He lifts himself off the bed and goes down to the dining room.

One large table has been laid to enable the whole party to eat together, Morris takes a place and scrutinises his fellow walkers, most still nameless. Jerry, now like a close friend in this group of strangers, makes a drinking gesture from across the table. Morris nods, and mouths 'red wine'.

The blond woman is sitting next to her friend, no partners in evidence. Snatches of their conversation he hears have the familiarity that suggests a long-standing friendship.

He takes a mouthful of wine as soon as the glass appears in front of him. Alcohol, he knows already, is no cure for his malaise, but his mood improves as the red wine enters his system. Alcohol, too, is having its organic effect around the table, lively conversations developing as glasses are emptied and replenished. 'Mark', the man sitting on the left introduces himself. Mark wears a neatly trimmed beard which has Morris thinking of Chaucer's *Marchant...with a forked beerd* . Morris gives his name but has no urge to enquire further of this man with lifeless eyes, turning to introduce himself to the youngish hennaed-haired woman on his right. 'Constance,' she replies, brightly, adding, as if needing to justify such a virtuous name, 'my mother's family were Quakers.' He tries to envisage her as the Prioress. Her eyes fitted, *eyen grey as glass,* but the capricious look she gives him does not accord with Chaucer's description, *hir smiling was full simple and coy.* He looks along the table to the blond woman. She lacks the heft and girth ascribed to the Wife of Bath, perhaps it would be better if that designation were applied to her more amply proportioned friend.

Dave, midway along the table, stands and clangs a

spoon against a glass water-jug.

'Welcome to Footloose—'

'And Fancy Free,' calls out a burly woman, repeating the company strap-line which appears on its literature. This brings uneasy, almost self-conscious laughter from around the table. It rekindles Morris's impression that the company's advertising is angled towards attracting people looking for a holiday where sexual adventures were likely. And didn't that lie behind his own reason in choosing Footloose?

Dave outlines the programme, explaining that they will be following the old pilgrim route to Santiago de Compostela: 'In the footsteps of the many thousands since the Middle Ages, who have made this pilgrimage to the tomb of the apostle St James,' he says. 'We will be going as far as Conques, your baggage transported ahead each day to the next hotel on our route.' Several people have questions about the accommodation to be provided. 'I expect to be able to meet particular needs for single or twin rooms most nights,' he assures.

Morris surveys his fellow pilgrims, his companions for the next fortnight, but his eyes keep returning to the striking blonde. When she and her friend get up from the table, he also leaves and returns to the solitude of his room.

2

He had told Pauline that he was leaving the job and going away. But where could he go? It was his wife's home town, Morris a relative newcomer: nearly all the people he knew were Gwen's friends. He had lost contact with people he'd known in the town where he grew up, and, since Greg had gone to Australia, there was no one he knew well enough to call upon at this critical time. Driven by an urgent need to get away, he phoned his mother to say he would be arriving the following day, cutting short her anxious questioning saying he would explain when he saw her.

The bungalow was as he remembered it on his one previous visit a year ago. Gwen and he had spent a few days staying with her friends in Brighton, and his parents had recently moved south to this place along the coast. Morris parked behind his dad's car, his own begrimed vehicle looking dilapidated next to such polished newness. The sound of a lawnmower greeted him from behind the bungalow and he found his father cutting the grass in a precise pattern of stripes. He saw Morris but didn't stop until he'd completed a section, his son waiting and already beginning to feel like a refractory teenager.

'Alice is inside,' said his father, and resumed his grass cutting. Morris made his way to the open French windows where his mother had appeared. She hugged him warmly.

'I'm glad to see you—whatever the reason for your visit.'

'Thanks, mum, I'm not bearing good tidings,' he said. 'But how are you keeping?'

'I'm fine—you don't have to worry about me.'

The sound of the lawnmower ceased and Morris braced himself for the coming encounter. Theirs had been a difficult and perplexing relationship, swinging precipitately from the adoration in early childhood, to a brittle oppositional attitude in adolescence. His father, who had worked his way up from collecting small insurance premiums door to door to becoming manager of the local branch, had been highly critical of what he considered to be his son's casual attitude to work and his wayward approach to life in general. Morris's poor results at university had provoked angry outbursts against idleness. The one aspect of his life that had his father's approval was Morris's choice of wife, Margaret a positive woman his dad admired, perhaps hoping that marriage to her would have an improving effect on his son. The divorce, with Morris the erring husband, only two years into the marriage, had been the final straw, and contact between father and son became almost non-existent. On the rare occasions when they were both present, usually family events connected with Morris's sister Karen, few words were exchanged between them. His mother did her best to keep the peace between father and son. She was never openly critical of Morris, not even reproaching him for the divorce, though he knew that she had hoped for grandchildren from his marriage and upset by the outcome.

'To what do we owe your presence?' His father stood in the doorway, formidable and intimidating.

'I needed to get away for a few days.'

'He can stay here as long as he wishes,' his mother said, addressing her husband with a firmness that Morris had not previously witnessed. The angry response he expected did not come.

'I suppose we will hear about the mess you're making of your life,' said his father.

A change had taken place in his parents' relationship, and Morris wondered if this had arisen from their different roles since his dad's retirement. He had lost his cherished status as branch manager and was no longer the working breadwinner. His wife, from her employment as a nurse at a care home, now the one working and earning. Morris drew strength from his mother's new assertiveness.

'Gwen and I have agreed on a temporary separation,' he told them.

'And how long is temporary?' his dad said, settling himself into a chair.

'I don't know—a month or two.'

'What about your job?' his mother wanted to know.

'I've taken leave—'

'—of your senses,' said his father.

'Edward!' reprimanded his mother. 'I'm going to make a meal,' she said, eying the two of them sitting in the room. Both rose immediately and offered to help.

'You stay in here Morris—you'll need a rest after that long drive.'

At this his dad hastened from the room and the immediate prospect of them being left together avoided.

Yet being left together became the regular situation of Morris's stay, his mother working most days at the care home. Morris thought that she must have spoken to her husband about his attitude to their son, for he found his dad to be more approachable than he had expected. He accepted Morris's offer of help in the garden, and welcomed his assistance with the painting and maintenance of the bungalow. A tacit agreement became established of starting the day by a discussion of the things that needed to be done. Soon they were doing tasks together. Morris realised that his father was lonely, a recognition of his own feeling.

His nights were disturbed by dreams of Pauline and she was rarely out of his mind during the day. If only Greg was still here, he could have released these pent-up feelings to his long-time friend as in the past, when in the habit of exchanging confidences about their life and loves over a beer. He knew by the concerned look she sometimes gave him, that his mother was aware his mind was troubled. There were times when he had to resist the temptation to respond by telling her about Pauline.

Often during the day, when not helping his dad, he filled the time by taking long walks on the Downs and by the sea. Returning one day Morris found his car being washed by his dad, an indication of how much had improved between them. It also brought an awareness of the extent he was becoming reabsorbed into his parents' life. He needed a change of scene, to make a break from this limbo-like existence: to live again an adult and sexual life.

In his hasty departure from the flat, he'd stuffed personal papers into one of his bags, relieved to find that his passport was among them. Still valid, it had been renewed just before his wedding to Gwen and their honeymoon in Venice. Scrutinising the passport revived memories of their delight in one another at that time, not so long ago. His photograph seemed to stare out at him accusingly, stirring feelings of remorse. What was wrong with him? First Margaret and now Gwen, each abandoned for a new love. But this is different, he told himself, Pauline is the love of his life, and now it was he who is suffering the anguish of rejection. Made no less painful in knowing that he had not been discarded for another lover, but sacrificed for the sake of her children.

Where should he go? The last time he had holidayed alone was at a New Age kind of place on a Greek island. Attracted there by the communal living and activities like learning to windsurf. It's where he met Gwen, a lively, bronzed sun goddess, who radiated an aura of sensual hippyness. From the start he'd been captivated, ecstatic when his feelings were returned with similar intensity. Unlike the suntans, their passion didn't fade after the holiday, and led to the Venice honeymoon and the passport he was examining. Yet there had been a fading, inevitable he supposed, though to his mind a factor was Gwen's single-minded desire to advance within the teaching profession—said it was her vocation. Her decision to move from the small cottage she'd had when he moved in with her was unexpected, but it was Gwen's choice of a larger, more conventional house, that curtailed his hopes of the freewheeling, carefree existence he had envisaged their life would be. The little capital he was left with after his divorce, and a good proportion of his monthly salary was needed to finance his stake in the property. Money was tight, but increasing his income by seeking promotion—Gwen's suggestion, had no appeal. He liked his work as an ordinary social worker, he told her, and had no wish to be engaged in management and administration. It would have meant the end of his close working with Pauline.

Going back to the Greek island would be like blowing on the ashes of a dead fire, and he continued his search for a suitable holiday. Lying on a beach or wandering about ancient buildings had no appeal: he decided on a walking holiday and came up with Footloose. He liked the idea of following a long-established pilgrim route, his interest arising from the Canterbury Tales' course. But it was Footloose's enticing blurb that clinched his decision, his imagination running ahead, picturing himself in the company of fit brown-legged women hikers in their tight shorts.

His dad insisted on driving him to Gatwick, and the happiness shown in his mother's face as he and his father drove off together, lingered in Morris's mind. After two months with his parents, the longest period since leaving university, he'd come to a better understanding of the man at the wheel than at any time in his life. It had also brought regret for what had been lost.

3

Morris is alone outside the hotel entrance, he sits on one of the metal chairs bordering the pavement. An empty coffee cup, the extent of his continental breakfast, is on a small table near him. He rolls a cigarette, occasionally glancing at the hotel doorway. He lights the thinly made cigarette, and inhales with a satisfying gasp.

He'd had a difficult night. Oppressed by the loneliness of his room, he went down to the bar for a drink. Several of the men from Footloose were there, but none of the women. 'Unpacking their damned clothes, I expect,' said John, whose manner and military moustache had Morris thinking of Chaucer's Knight. Though not *a veray, parfit gentil knight,* judging by his abrasive attitude to hotel staff. With him was a young man whose hair formed a dense covering of tight black curls. He seemed out of place on this holiday, and Morris had wondered why someone so young, mid-twenties at most, would choose to be with an aging group like Footloose. 'My son, Simon,' said John.

Communal drinking with a group of men had never had much attraction for Morris, he not a man who had ever adopted a 'local', or the attendant habit of regularly meetings with drinking acquaintances. Against the enormity of his loss the conversation of the Footloose men around him seemed banal, their concerns trivial. He finished his beer and bid them goodnight, had then lain awake with his tormenting thoughts of Pauline.

Members of the Footloose group are now coming out of the hotel, and Morris takes a quick draw on the thin cigarette. Jerry comes and sits by him.

'I wondered why you were in such a hurry to get out—it's the weed.'

'I gave it up years ago—recent events set me going again. Would you like a roll-up?'

'I've never smoked,' says Jerry. 'What are you doing about lunch?'

'Can't we get a bite on the way?'

'Dave says there's nowhere on today's route—we'll need to take a picnic. I'm off to get something now. You coming?'

'After I've finished my smoke.'

'What do you want? I can get it.'

'Just bread and some slices of ham—oops sorry, make that cheese.'

'Don't worry, I'm Jewish but have no religion. I'll bring you a bacon sandwich if you like,' Jerry says, smiling.

'I'll have what you're having—be simplest.'

He watches Jerry going along the street, feels encouraged by this quick holiday friendship. Others of the group are coming out of the hotel, acknowledging him as they pass onto the street. The blond woman gives him a smile as her steely blue eyes pass over him. 'We're going to get something for our lunches,' says her companion. Constance pauses by him: in day light her hair has a gingery glow, and he notices pale freckles on her nose. She eyes his cigarette.

'You look like a man who could rustle up a spliff in an emergency.'

'I get enough of a hit from tobacco,' he tells her.

She looks at him disbelieving, and carries on into the street.

A large man with a ginger beard, his paunch barely contained within his wide shorts, sinks onto a nearby chair.

'You're someone who won't mind me lighting up—it's hard to have a fag these days without somebody making a fuss.' He takes a squashed pack from the taut pocket of his shorts. 'Twenty-four kilometres—how far's that?'

'About fifteen miles,' Morris tells him.

'Jesus! This was my wife's idea.'

'Which is your wife?'

'Oh, she's not come. You're getting too fat—out of condition she says. Been on at me a while to take more exercise. I have to agree with her,' looking down at his bulging waistband. 'Jim Wilson,' he says, and Morris, introducing himself, thinks of Chaucer's Miller.

'Go on one of those hiking holidays,' she said. 'I wasn't keen, though when I saw this one, walking a bit each day from hotel to hotel, refreshment and food waiting, bags carried for you—I thought, that'll do for me. But I hadn't reckoned on fifteen miles.'

'Did you not get details of the route?'

'I didn't give the distances much thought till now. I'd better go and get some grub to take if I'm to survive. Have you got yours?'

'Jerry's bringing mine.'

'The little guy—I should have asked one of the lasses to get me something.'

The Miller, Morris can't think of him in any other way, stubs out his cigarette and heaves himself up from the creaking chair.

Jerry returns and occupies the chair where Jim Wilson had been sitting.

'I got some pasties and some delicious looking fruit tarts from a boulangerie. Also bought some peaches—keep the scurvy at bay.' He passes one of the two bags he is holding.

'Thanks Jerry—what do I owe you?'

'Your turn tomorrow.'

'Did you see our Miller on the street?'

'What? Oh! I certainly did. I thought he was one of ours, with his pink knees and white legs. *Full big he was of brawn and eek of bones...his beerd as any sow or fox was red.* I wonder what his real occupation is?'

'Something sedentary—truck driver.'

'Or running a fast-food place and eating the profits,' Jerry suggests.

They go into the hotel to prepare for the first day's hike.

Mid-morning, under a blue sky and in bright sun, the group are moving through open country, walking mainly in twos and threes spread out behind Dave. Morris is almost at the end of the line, a deliberate choice which enables him to observe the pilgrims, as he thinks of his fellow hikers. Almost all are in shorts, as is he: most of the women and a few of the men walking with poles, some using two. Occasionally mobile phones are produced, not for telephoning as this is discouraged during the walks, but to take photographs.

He didn't feel rejected when Jerry said that he wanted to circulate and get to know others in the group, the same intention also in Morris's mind. Jerry, he sees, is talking to the blond woman, whose regular companion is engaged in conversation with another man. He envies Jerry's luck; his own walking partner is the Miller.

'Nobody else seems to smoke, and I could do with a fag,' he'd said, coming up to Morris, and pulling out his crushed packet. 'Do you want one?'

'I'm trying stick to just one after meals,' Morris tells him, 'but go ahead, your smoke won't bother me.'

'What kind of car do you run?' he asks, after taking a draw on his cigarette.

'A Citroën,' Morris surprised by the question.

'They're buggers to work on, Citroens. I'm in the motor trade—me and my brother. We started off in the used-car business. Our first agency for new was with Skoda, back when they were still a bit of a joke. That all changed when Volkswagen took them over. What's your line of work, Morris?'

'I'm a social worker.'

'What the fuck *is* a social worker? I've never understood what they do.'

'I'm not always sure myself.'

The Miller plods on alongside, the cigarette hanging in his mouth, his eyes on the walkers ahead.

'There's some handsome women here,' he says, the burning stub dropping from his lips.

4

The Host, as Morris now looks upon Dave, calls a halt for lunch, guides the walkers onto a grassy slope bordered by woodland. Morris slips off his backpack and flops down onto the grass. The Miller, who has accompanied him for the past hour, continues on into the trees, gesturing an urgent need. Jerry comes and sits by him, and they each delve into their packs, producing their identical picnics.

'She's a widow,' says Jerry.

'Who?' Morris knowing full well who.

'Diana...the blond woman you can't keep your eyes off.'

'She is very attractive. What's the story with her friend?'

'They're not a female couple if that's what you're thinking. She met Helen on their first day at university and have been close friends ever since. Through thick and thin, she says. Her bereavement and Helen's divorces.'

'She's a widow?' Morris is incredulous.

'Yes.'

'Young to be a widow,' he says, staring at the woman as if expecting to see evidence of this condition. 'And her friend's divorced?'

'The Wife of Bath?' Jerry says, bringing a smile from Morris. 'At least twice from what Diana told me, one fairly recent, but apparently it hasn't put Helen off marriage. It's amazing how readily people open up when walking together.'

'Yes,' says Morris, with some bitterness, looking to where Diana lies stretched out on the grass. 'The Miller has told me about his motor business.'

This man now emerges towards them from the trees, changes direction when he sees Morris is not alone, and makes for a woman who is lighting a cigarette.

'How long has she been a widow?'

Jerry gives him a searching look, and smiles.

14

'I'll make way for you after lunch...you shall have an opportunity to learn more of the lovely widow.'

'I'm embarrassed now, not two days and you know me better than do my colleagues. God knows what you will have learned by the time we finish this holiday,' Morris says cheerfully, relishing the prospect of having a confidante, a friend he could share his feelings with, even for just a fortnight.

'I want to spend two weeks freed from context, avoiding reference to the life left behind, or thinking of the one awaiting,' Jerry declares.

'Is that possible?' Morris's smile fading.

'Hold curiosity at bay, and resist the urge to confess,' asserts Jerry.

'I think we need to get out of this hot sun,' says the social worker.

They are on the move again, Morris and Jerry walking together and positioned not far behind Diana and Helen.

'I'll go and engage the Wife of Bath—give you a chance to make your pitch to her blond friend. Good luck,' and Jerry strides forward.

Morris watches his astute friend as he approaches Helen. The two are soon lodged in conversation—this is his chance. He hesitates, suddenly tense and nervous, forces himself onwards, unwilling to risk incurring Jerry's contempt for a lack of resolve.

'Hello, I'm Morris,' his voice sounding squeaky.

'I know,' she says. 'I've felt your eyes on me—I asked Jerry your name.'

'It's your hair,' he says, blushing, 'it's so...so striking.'

'You attracted to blondes?'

This was not the time to explain about the black-haired Pauline.

'Not particularly.'

'Is your wife blond?'

'I'm separated,' he says, quickly adopting this designation. 'She rang the changes with hair colour.'

'What brought you on this holiday?' Her sharp blue eyes searching his face.

'Chaucer, The Canterbury Tales.'

'That's what Jerry said. I didn't believe him either. We did Chaucer at school but it had no bearing on the choice of holiday. I came for sunshine, good food and wine, walking through pleasant country, and perhaps meeting interesting people.'

The last is said with a wide smile, softening her inquisitorial eyes. God, she is beautiful he thinks as they walk together in the French countryside.

'Those things too,' he concedes.

'And to get away from the routine of work—an annual break for hedonism. What do you do?'

'I'm a social worker. And you?'

'I tell people I'm at an Oxford College, which is true, though my job is fairly mundane admin. How long have you known your lawyer friend?'

'Since the start of this holiday.'

She shows surprise: 'We—I thought you already knew one another.'

'I can't remember when I last holidayed alone,' he says.

'Usually with your wife and children, I expect.'

'Yes,' says Morris, deciding against any elaboration of his family situation. 'Jerry tells me you are a widow. It must have been distressing to lose a husband so early in life.'

'Like you we were separated— it spared the necessity of a divorce.'

'He didn't...?'

'No, not by his own hand. The hand of God perhaps,' she says, giving a tight smile.

'The children?'

'We never got round to having children,' her voice losing some of its assurance.

They walk for a few minutes in silence, until she says, with her former assertiveness: 'There will be other opportunities to chat.'

Dismissed, he drops back, and is replaced by Helen who had been at his heels.

'How did you get on with the fair Diana?' Jerry asks, when they are again walking together.

'We could have a female Manciple—she's involved in the management of a college.'

'Not much progress in your suit, then? The Wife of Bath was asking a lot of questions about you. I guess she's on the lookout for husband number three. She'd be wasting her time with a Nun, perhaps you should become the Monk, *A manly man, to been an abbot able.*'

5

Hot and tired from the steep sections of the route, Morris is glad to have finally arrived at the small hillside village, the day's destination. The Footloose walkers are strung out along the street following Dave as he leads them to their accommodation. Anticipating the bliss of a refreshing shower, Morris quickens his step at the thought that such facilities may be in short supply at this village hotel. He is relieved to find that the room he is sharing with Jerry has an ensuite shower, and Jerry, collapsing onto his bed, nods his agreement to Morris having first go. He luxuriates in the hot water streaming down over his body, his fatigued limbs reviving.

Revigorated by the shower, and freshened by a shave, his thoughts turn to the coming evening. From the few clothes with him he selects a clean shirt and puts on lightweight trousers, checks himself in the mirror. A few grey hairs among the ample brown: looks young for his age, he thinks.

'I fancy a drink,' he says to Jerry, who, rising from his bed, mumbles something about being down later.

Morris arrives in the hotel lounge at the same time as the waiter bearing a tray of drinks for the several Footloose guests already gathered there. Among them is the Miller, who immediately drinks off his glass of beer, and orders another. Standing with him is Mark, the Merchant, who sips a gin and tonic. Morris orders a beer and approaches Peter, an older, weathered looking man who is standing alone holding a milky glass of pastis.

'I've done a lot of sailing in the Med—got a taste for ouzo in Greece, and this stuff in France,' he says, lifting up his glass.

'In Greece I've drunk retsina, yet hardly touched any I brought back. Tastes different under grey skies,' says Morris, keeping a discreet watch on the doorway for any sign of Diana.

'I miss the sun and heat,' says Peter, who Morris decides will be the Shipman. *He knew all the havens as they were Fro Gotland to the Cape of Finistere.*

Diana and Helen appear, Morris moves from Peter and greets the two women.

'Can I get you a drink?' he says, looking at Diana.

'A gin and tonic—lemon and ice,' replies Helen.

'Very kind of you,' says Diana, 'it's her favourite tipple.'

'And for yourself—?'

'Ah! Jerry,' she says, her eyes looking beyond Morris to the approaching man. 'Your friend is offering us drinks.'

'A beer for me,' he says, giving Morris a knowing look.

'And I would like a Kir,' says Diana.

They stand waiting for their drinks, chat about the day's walking. Morris is dismayed to see that Diana is giving most of her attention to Jerry. It is Helen who is showing interest in himself. He studies the Wife of Bath, inevitably comparing this big-hipped, brown-haired woman with Pauline. Helen becomes blotted out as visions of Pauline swamp his mind. He has to forget her; must exorcise the haunting blackness of her hair in the arms of a golden-haired goddess. Depressed by the little progress he is making in achieving this end, his mind veers away from the unpromising developments all too apparent around him, speculates instead on the kind of charged emotional exchanges likely to be radiating wilfully beneath the bland chit-chat, in silent and hidden communication. Morris surfaces from this escape into abstraction when he sees Constance coming into the room. She pauses to look around before deciding to join the four of them, and greets everyone just as the waiter arrives with the drinks.

'What would you like?' Morris having abandoned any hope of trying to keep his spending within limits.

'Thanks— I'd love a white wine,' her grey eyes giving him a look he finds mystifying.

With a feeling of having become the host of this little

group, he makes an effort to include Constance in their discussions. The other two women, Helen particularly, showing a marked coolness towards this new arrival. Talk becomes scant, often barbed, as drinks are sipped in the wait for the hour of dinner. Constance shows little sign of being intimidated by the attitude of Diana and her friend.

The Knight and Simon enter. *'With him there was his son, a yong Squier, A lover and a lusty bacheler,'* Jerry murmurs to Morris. The appearance of a handsome young man among this collection of aging males, draws the eyes of the women. Simon shows no reaction to this blatant interest, as if accustomed to receiving such attention. Not so his father, John strutting and preening as if he too was an object of desire. The hotel lounge becomes filled with hungry hikers glancing at their watches, and when the time comes, no one hangs back from the concerted move to the dining room. In the hasty arrival at the dinner table Morris finds himself seated between Helen and Jerry, who has Diana on his left. Constance is further along, on the other side of the long table. He struggles to make conversation with Helen, constrained by her close physical presence. She is, she tells him, the manager of the Citizens Advice Bureau in a London borough.

'Both of us attracted to helping people,' she exclaims, and he assumes that Diana has told her that he is a social worker.

'I don't have a job at present,' he adds quickly, seeking to lessen his acceptability.

'There are always vacancies for social workers,' she says emphatically.

This is a purposeful woman, he realises, who will not be easily shaken off.

'Let's get some wine,' he says to Jerry, breaking into his friend's conversation with Diana.

The drink and food ease Morris's discomfort, and his attitude to Helen becomes less defensive. The time at the table passes fairly sociably, but he is ready for a calvados with his coffee. The two women leave together. Jerry opts for cognac.

'The Wife of Bath has got you in her sights,' he says.

'And the blond Manciple is after you.'

'Diana is on the hunt for a husband, but not for herself. They are working together with one object in mind—a new husband for Helen.'

'Why me—and not you?'

'And the way left open for a dalliance with your blond heartthrob? By your own admission you are separated and thus available.'

'For all I know you're not even married.'

'They are working on what they know—these two canny women.'

'You and Diana seem to hit it off.'

'I suspect I'm being used to block off your interest in her—divert your attention to the needs of her friend.'

'Friendships between women are more elemental than men's,' sighs Morris.

6

'I'm staying with my parents whilst looking for somewhere to buy in Brighton—their home is within easy reach,' Morris tells Constance, who walks alongside.

'Brighton's great—I was at university there,' she says, a distant look in her eyes.

'London by the sea,' he says.

'I'd thought about staying on in Brighton…'

'Accommodation's expensive,' Morris probing for the reason she left.

'Very,' her grey eyes again on him. 'What sort of place are you looking for?'

'A flat I suppose—a two-bedroom flat,' he decides, and quickly changes the subject. 'How did you come to choose this holiday? Is walking this route a kind of pilgrimage?'

'Good God, no! Do you know anything about Compostela and St Jacques?'

'I know very little about saints. Was he responsible for Spain becoming Christian?'

'He was celebrated as Saint James the Moor-Slayer—became associated with the expulsion of Muslims and Jews from Spain. The end of hundreds of years of religious tolerance. Hardly a man any Quaker could revere.'

'Jerry is Jewish—I wonder if he's aware of all this.'

'Strange for a Jew to be here.'

'Or a Quaker,' he grins.

'Did you ever see the TV series about *The Canterbury Tales*? Set in modern times but following the same pilgrimage route.'

'I must have missed that,' his interest heightened.

'It was some years ago—back in more halcyon days. A time that was in my mind when I booked this holiday. I amuse myself on the trail by matching people here to those Canterbury pilgrims.'

'Who am I?' he asks, intrigued by Constance's revelation.

'The Sergeant of the Law in the TV series has a tale about a girl called Constance.'

'Jerry would be our Man of Law—he's a solicitor,' says Morris, discouraged.

'Sometimes I imagine I'm on a horse—have to stop myself from trotting,' she grins.

'The Prioress riding to Canterbury—*eyen grey as glass*,' he says.

'So you know *The Canterbury Tales,* too,' her eyes shining.

'It adds to the interest of the holiday,' he says.

'I'm going to gallop on ahead—The Prioress needs a word with Mary, she's a psychologist; there are things I wish to ask her.'

Morris sees Constance catch up with a woman about his own age, whose cropped hair is a distinctive grey. He walks on alone, his mind occupied by thoughts of the uncanny encounter with Constance. He looks for the blond Manciple but she is not among the walkers visible in this woody stretch.

They are stopped for lunch at a village café, most of the pilgrims sitting outside. Morris is with Jerry at one of the tables inside the café, telling him of his earlier meeting with Constance.

'She turned the tables on me, did the Prioress. We're not the only ones playing this game of matching people to Canterbury pilgrims. She seems slightly mad.'

'And what we are doing is the epitome of male sanity?' Jerry says, with a mocking grin.

'At least we don't imagine we're on horseback or...' he breaks off when he sees Constance coming into the café. She joins them at the table.

'I don't know what I've done but that Helen woman is quite frosty with me.'

'The Wife of Bath,' says Jerry.

'You guys are worse than me with this Canterbury thing. In the BBC production she was a TV actress who'd had several husbands, had just been left by the latest one, and on the lookout for the next.'

'Helen is not long divorced,' says Morris.

'I've never actually been married.'

'It would not be expected of a Prioress,' says Jerry.

7

'Constance has been telling me about the Saint James who led to this becoming a pilgrimage route,' says Morris, as he and Jerry walk together in the direction of the distant shrine. 'Was known as Saint James the Moor-Slayer, and became associated with the expulsion of Muslims and Jews from Spain. Did you know any of this?'

'Not really—though I understand there was a period in Spain during the early Middle Ages which is seen as a Jewish Golden Age, Jews having many more rights under the Moors than in a Christian Europe. I came on this holiday because the thought of walking like this through the French countryside seemed just what I needed. If I wanted to avoid places that have some association with the persecution of Jews, where is there to go? I'm not put off visiting York because of the pogrom there in the fourteenth century.'

'Constance got quite heated about St James.'

'A contrast to Chaucer's Prioress whose tale was of the murder of a small boy for singing a Christian song as he walked to school through the Ghetto. *There was in Asie in a greet citee, amonges Christen folk, a Jewerye, Sustened by a lord of that contree for foul usure and lucre of villainye.* The Jews deemed responsible for his death were torn apart by wild horses. I found it painful to read, to be faced with the intensity of antisemitism in Chaucer's time.'

'I couldn't imagine our Prioress telling such a tale, she so passionate in condemning the way Jews were treated by the Christian King Ferdinand.

'If only everyone were good like Constance,' a troubled look clouding Jerry's face.

This sudden change in his friend's usual cheerful expression has Morris wondering what Jerry was leaving behind. Was he, too, driven here in an effort to come to terms with an emotional crisis? It was frustrating of him to insist on maintaining a blanket over his life, and discouraging any discussion of what was lying out there for either of them. Almost from the beginning the overwhelming intensity of his affair with Pauline had led to a growing need to confide in someone. But there had been no one, no close friend he could go to. Here in France, away from people who knew him, he would willingly have opened up his heart to Jerry, and breathe life into his remembrance of her; Pauline reified in this emotional exposure.

Jerry's face clears, and his cheerful look returns. Morris, scrutinising his friend for any sign which might herald a revision in Jerry's attitude to revelations about his life, senses the defensive reticence in Jerry's make-up.

Morris makes it to the hotel dining room just in time for the start of dinner. Allocated a single room that night he'd stretched out on the bed and fallen asleep. With no companion to wake him he slept through the time he'd intended to join the others for a drink. In a panic, with time only for a quick shower, rushed and feeling dishevelled, he'd hurried down to the dining room. He lurches onto an empty seat at the table just as Diana arrives and takes the adjacent chair. His goddess next to him! Morris breathes deeply in an effort to steady himself, wishing to make the most of her close presence, regretting he'd not had time to shave.

Diana is talking to Helen who is sitting on her other side. What would he say when her attention comes his way? Before he has gathered his words, Diana turns to him, and asks: 'Which one am I?'

'Which...?' he wavers

'I know what you and your friend are up to, Helen got it out of him—her Chaucerian identity. She did The Canterbury Tales at school; her favourite character happened to be the Wife of Bath—so who am I?'

'The Manciple,' he admits nervously.

'What? A man!' Her voice rising in protest. 'Do you

see me as being masculine?'

'Oh no! Never! It's because of your position at the college—a bit like that of Chaucer's Manciple.'

'I assume Jerry is the Sergeant at the Law, but who are you?'

'The Monk,' he tells her, encouraged by the unprecedented interest she is showing.

'And do you have a tale to tell?' Her radiant blue eyes fixing on him.

'I'm sure we all have,' he murmurs, encompassed within her hypnotic gaze.

'Who else have you named?'

'The Shipman, the Oxford Cleric—'

'The Shipman, yes! But the Oxford Cleric?'

'Thomas, the older, academic looking man— always has a book with him at the dinner table. *Of study took he most cure and most heed. Not oo word spak he more than was need.* And there's—'

'We could have our own tales,' she breaks in, 'The Footloose Tales. I was disappointed that Chaucer's pilgrims told stories unrelated to themselves. The Footloose Tales should be more biographical,' she declares, as if to clinch the whole project.

'Yes,' he says, wondering what his story could be. And there's Jerry with his reluctance to speak about his life beyond Footloose?

'Who are you thinking of?'

'The four of us already named.'

'There's also Constance,' he says, bringing a slackening of Diana's gaze. 'I wouldn't want to leave her out—she seems quite isolated,' he adds, feeling a need to explain.

Diana turns to her friend and tells her of The Footloose Tales. 'Isn't it a great idea,' says Helen, leaning forward to speak to Morris. He nods his response.

Jerry shows no enthusiasm for Footloose Tales when Morris tells him of what Diana, abetted now by Helen, is proposing.

'What? Narrate them as we walk along?'

'Diana doesn't think that would work— it will be after dinner in the hotel.'

'I used to wonder how Chaucer's pilgrims delivered their stories; he gives the impression that they will be told as they ride along. *Now let us ride, and herkneth what I saye,"* his Knight says. *And with that word we ridden forth our waye. And he began with right a mirry cheere. His tale anon, and said as you may heere.* Yet who out of the twenty-odd horsemen would be able to hear? I guess it's a case of suspending disbelief.'

'One of us is to tell a story each evening.'

'I'll go last—give me time to think up something.'

'You'll have to take a chance on that—the evening's story-teller is to be selected randomly, by choosing cards. And Diana says we should tell our stories like Chaucer's pilgrims, and avoid reading from notes.

'These women are taking charge,' groans Jerry, downing the rest of his cognac.

In the morning Morris seeks out Constance as the pilgrims set off, tells her of Footloose Tales as they walk together.

'I'm really happy to be included. I'd better start to think of a story.'

'I don't have a clue what I'm going to talk about,' says Morris.

In the evening the five members of Footloose Tales cluster together at the dinner table, the meal eaten in an atmosphere of hushed expectation, Jerry unusually quiet. The group attracting frequent glances from others at the table. The meal over, the five gather in a quiet corner of the hotel, their chairs drawn up closely together. Diana produces a set of cards.

'I don't have a story ready,' says Constance.

'Me neither,' says Morris.

'We need a day or two to prepare,' Jerry says.

'I agree,' adds Helen.'

'Tomorrow—we'll start tomorrow,' Diana declares.

Morris lies awake mulling over ideas for a tale; there must be something in his social work experience that would make a good story. Eddie! There was more than enough in his dealings with Eddie for a Footloose tale. He is finally able to sleep.

8

Morris and several others from Footloose, are in a small circular chapel alongside the pilgrim route. Thomas, his eyes shining within the cool and shaded interior of its thick walls, in a sudden transition from his usual silence, is regaling his fellow walkers with an animated exposition of twelfth-century Romanesque chapels: 'A style of architecture that signified the emergence of medieval Europe from the dark-ages,' he pronounces. The Oxford Cleric is still in full flow when Morris and Jerry emerge from beneath the chapel's rounded arches into the bright heat of day. *'Souning in moral virtue was his speech; And gladly wold he lern and gladly teeche.'* says Jerry.

A stranger follows them out of the chapel, a bearded, sun-burnished man bearing a sizable backpack. '*Guten Morgen,*' he says.

'*Guten...Tag,*' Morris responds.

'*Sehr erfreut,*' says Jerry.

'Ah, you are English, which I well speak. My name is Gunter. I walk to Compostela. Are you going there also?'

'Just as far as Conques,' says Jerry.

'I go also to Conques for mass at the cathedral.'

'We are not proper pilgrims,' says Morris.

'Proper? What is 'proper'?' Gunter asks.

'It's a walking holiday— we're not real pilgrims,' says Jerry.

'The Professor speaking in the chapel, he is not a holy man,' the German says.

Gunter, using a wooden staff, walks with them along the broad track, silent after the initial exchange. Walking by the side of this pious pilgrim Morris feels like a profane imposter, each step a desecration of hallowed ground, the Footloose holiday a frivolous utilisation of this sanctified route. He searches for something to say, but it is Gunter who breaks the silence. 'One month have I been walking, I am starting at Ulm.'

'At night—where do you sleep?'

'I have a *credential*, the pass from my church to give me places to sleep for little money.' He takes a document from an inner pocket, and unfolds it. Morris sees that it bears the stamp of each place where Gunter has stayed. There are many blank spaces yet to be filled.

'A long way to go,' says Morris.

'After two more months I shall be getting my *compostela* certificate at Santiago. I shall go to the Pilgrim's Mass in the cathedral.'

'Why are you making this pilgrimage?' Jerry asks.

Gunter is silent, giving Morris the impression that he doesn't wish to discuss the reason. Jerry looks as though he is about to repeat his question when Gunter speaks. 'Each day walking I do much thinking, but not speaking. My words stay inside me,' he pauses as if in need of air. 'I was child in East Berlin, I knew only what was taught—at school it was Russian, no English. America and the West our enemies. My work was at the *Berliner Mauer,* the Wall. Shoot people trying to cross—they are criminals, we are told. When the wall came down my *Grundstock* also was destroyed.'

'Foundations,' says Jerry, responding to Morris's questioning look.

'For many there was no happiness. I was living in darkness. Would I be punished for what I had done when a guard? At night bad memories were in my dreams. I did not have hope. I was saved by a priest, who led me to Christ. The Church became my *Grundstock,* but prayer alone does not bring forgiveness. There must be an act of atonement also.'

'So this pilgrimage...?'

'Yes! Many years have I waited. When I reach Santiago de Compostela and receive my *certificate* my penance will be completed.'

In front of them the main Footloose contingent has halted for a picnic lunch, settling themselves on the ground, unwrapping food and opening flasks and bottles.

'Join us,' says Morris, 'we have plenty of food and drink.'

'*Danke vielmals*, but to reach the hostel I must keep walking.'

Morris and Jerry stand watching Gunter as he plods steadily onwards. 'Towards his redemption— I hope he is not disappointed,' Morris envying a man with a belief that walking this trail would atone for his sins.

'He's probably got most of the benefit from this pilgrimage already; his personal project whose years of anticipation will have given new meaning to his life.' says Jerry, settling himself in the shade of a tree.

'Just as well he didn't meet Constance with her talk of St James the Moor Killer. I wish him well and he gets the *compostela* certificate he is set on.'

'Completing the pilgrimage will bring its own problems. How does he fill the void that has opened up in his life?'

'Better than having to abandon the pilgrimage— breaking a leg, say?'

'Not necessarily, he would still have his project of completing the pilgrimage.'

'Are you saying that failure can be preferable to success?'

'In some cases, yes.'

9

'Ace high, lowest card kicks off,' says Diana, dealing each of them a playing card.

'Nine,' says Morris. Surely someone will get a lower card and he won't be called on to deliver his half-formed story tonight.

'I've got the Queen,' announces Helen.

'Mine's a ten,' comes from Constance.

Morris gazes at the pack in Diana's hand, imagines all the aces and face cards poised to precipitate him into telling his uncompleted tale.

'Seven,' says Jerry, softly.

Morris unwinds.

'Six,' says Diana, and Jerry's face brightens.

'My idea, so perhaps it's appropriate that I am the one who begins,' says Diana, to her now relaxed companions. She waits, in this quiet hotel room, until each of them is seated and settled, and she has their attention.

'I'm calling my Footloose Tale, Birth of a Manciple,' she announces.

'My vision of pursuing an academic career after university quickly fragmented when confronted by the hard realities of life. Money was needed and money was to be had in the commercial world, the sole reason why I subsequently became a high-end corporate events manager. Working wild hours, mainly in London, but could be anywhere in the country. A life arranging plush-covered gatherings of the well-connected. A world inhabited by rail-thin women teetering in black sheath dresses, kitted out with the required accoutrements of fashion. And trophy wives, fraught over their appearance, their expensively whitened teeth flashing as regular as lighthouses. And always, from those for whom the event has been arranged, speeches about improvement of some kind or other, delivered with a passion by individuals, who face to face had difficulty raising a smile.

Rushing between locations one day, the car came off the road on a bend, tearing through a roadside hedge and coming to rest in long meadow grass. I'd been too surprised to feel fear. Badly shaken but unhurt, I scrambled out and stood leaning on the scarred BMW, looking back in disbelief at the flattened greenery. When I had control of my limbs I recovered my phone and contacted the recovery service. Sitting on soft grass in the warm sun, I waited. It was peaceful in the meadow behind the broken hedge, listening to the sound of birdsong in the air. Black and white cattle grazed in the next field, and beyond a red tractor moved steadily across ploughed land. My frenzied life beyond the penetrated hedge became distanced and suddenly of little consequence.

Then I saw them! Raising my eyes to the skyline, appearing like a revelation, the spires of Oxford. Was I dreaming? Then I really was dreaming, the vision reawakening long abandoned hopes of an academic life. Into my fevered fantasising, the trundling recovery truck came as an unwelcome intrusion, dragging the car back onto the road, me trudging along behind.

"Lucky you missed the tree," remarked the driver.

I hadn't noticed the tall oak rising out of the hedge, its solid trunk hidden in hawthorn. A yard to the right...I'd been spared for better things, and I turned around to look again at those inviting spires on the horizon. But without the necessary academic qualifications what chance had I of gaining entrance into the world of an Oxford college?

The answer was my experience in the organisation and administration of conferences and events, not to enable me to take an academic post, but that of Domestic Bursar, today's more prosaic term for Manciple. Yet essentially having a similar function, responsible for managing the accommodation and feeding the students and staff of the College. In practice overseeing the heads of numerous departments, ranging from the JCR Bar Steward to the Head of Housekeeping. My day could start by receiving a phone call about a blocked toilet, and end with an on-site discussion about health and safety with the building contractor carrying out the College's multimillion pound development. Or, such are the ironies of life, discussing a forthcoming event with the Conference & Events Manager.

I sometimes wonder about the workings of fate, and a car that crashed at a place where the Oxford skyline could be seen. Such events are considered to be random, purely a matter of chance, though I have a fondness for the Ancient Greek idea that they arise from the intervention of one of their Gods. It's strange to think of a lucky car crash, but that is what led me to a worthwhile occupation and the return of my self-respect.'

Morris, who had listened with intent interest, keen to hear of anything that his goddess would reveal of herself, suppressed an urge to applaud. Compliments came from others in the group, bringing the fear that his own tale would be seen as a poor thing in comparison.

'I'm looking forward to what you're going to tell us,' Helen says to him, adding to his discomposure.

No one moves, and there is little conversation, Morris believes, that like him, they are each engrossed in their own biographies, wondering which aspect or incident could match up to the standard set by Diana's accomplished opener. She and Helen are the first to leave. Constance's eyes follow them but she remains seated. 'Do either of you do yoga?' she asks.

'I've tried it,' says Jerry.

'I've done a bit,' Morris says, wondering if her tale is going to be about yoga.

'I teach yoga.'

Morris glances at her, and imagines her lithe body contorted in some yoga pose.

'It's my main business but the income isn't great—I can barely afford this holiday. Not like some of the women here who must be loaded—the expensive gear and clothes they have.'

'Men too,' says Morris, 'everything Michael is kitted out in is top of the range.'

'The Doctor of Physic,' says Jerry: '*And yet he was but esy of dispense. He kepte that he won in pestilence; For gold in physic is a cordial—Therefore he loved gold in special.* Chaucer's Doctor is tight with money, and rich from the gold he's made from outbreaks of plague.'

'I didn't know Michael was a doctor,' she says.

'If you were a GP on holiday you'd keep it quiet too, unless you wanted to have a surgery every night.'

Constance rises from her chair. 'I need time to meditate on my story.'

'Me too,' Morris says.

'These damned tales,' says Jerry, 'I can't free my mind. We've all become emmeshed in the web of the blond spider.'

10

Morris lies awake trying to concentrate on the Footloose tale he will tell, but it is the untold story of Pauline that surges through his veins, and agitates his heart. She follows him into sleep, inhabits his dreams. Restless, he wakes early, and desperate for a smoke quietly dresses, Jerry sound asleep in the other bed, silent and still as an effigy. He goes out into the cool dawn, wanders along the empty street, sucking in nicotine. Two cigarettes later he is back in the hotel for coffee, edgy and irritable.

'I wondered where you'd got to,' says Jerry.

'Couldn't sleep.'

'Not getting to you is it—this Footloose Tales caper?'

'My story's shit.'

'I've managed to get something together,' Jerry sounding relaxed and confident. 'You might be on tonight,' he adds, with a grin.

Morris drinks his coffee in silence.

He walks alone much of the day. He avoids Jerry, irritated by his friend's sudden smugness, his own ideas no nearer to providing a satisfactory story. Constance joins him for a time, but says little as they walk, her thoughts seem elsewhere. Later in the day Morris almost welcomes the company of the Miller.

'Saw you had no one with you—thought you might like a smoke,' he says, producing a blue Gitanes pack. 'Don't know what you think of these? I'll smoke anything if needs be.'

'Thanks,' Morris takes a cigarette, his intention to limit his smoking already well breached.

'There's something up with Dave,' says the Miller. 'He's not the bright and breezy tour leader we started off with—you'd think he was carrying the weight of the world on his shoulders. I can hardly get a word out of him.'

'I hadn't noticed,' Morris says, drawing gingerly on his Gitane.

'What's your little gang about?'

'Oh...that! We're copying the Canterbury Pilgrims, each telling our own story.'

'There's a few good yarns I could tell,' the Miller says, stated as a fact, without any suggestion of proffering himself for inclusion.

Morris's gloom deepens, everyone, it seems, had a good story to tell.

At dinner he eats little and hardly speaks, his mind engaged in a frantic race to assemble a passable tale before he is called upon to deliver, feeling sure that it will be this evening. The group establish themselves on a tight circle of chairs in the lounge. Morris sits stiff and rigid with growing apprehension as the cards are dealt. His body slackens and he relaxes in the chair when it is Jerry who gets the lowest card. Jerry starts almost immediately, and Morris sits up, eager not to miss anything his cagey friend might reveal of his background.

'This is not my first walking holiday,' Jerry tells them, 'I went on one several years ago. I have no natural inclination for walking in the countryside and had to be persuaded. You look pale, unhealthy, I was told, and need a break, somewhere warm and sunny, with broader horizons. But I'm an urban person, my skyline shaped by buildings, happy to do my walking on streets and pavements. The pressure to take that holiday was sustained and I eventually acquiesced, feeling some obligation to respond to the concerns expressed for my well-being.'

He pauses, becoming conscious of Morris's fixed gaze, responds with a brief smile, and resumes.

'From the first day it was clear that Josephine was a gambler.

"How many leckies do you guess?" I overheard her say at breakfast.

"Twelve," said her friend Dorothy.

"Twenty euros says there will be more," said Josephine, crushing the top of a boiled egg.

Her friend sipped coffee thoughtfully. "You're on," she

said.

Ramblers! I thought. What am I doing amongst people who speak in code. Sitting outside in the warm sunshine of a Mallorcan September, I had no wish to go walking. That notion, which had been nurtured in a wet English spring, was wilting in this Mediterranean heat. Our leader appeared—too late to escape now. He was a bronzed and blond, athletic looking young man. From his accent I had him down as a Kiwi.

"Your country produces some great wine," I offered ingratiatingly.

"What do you mean?" An alarmed expression on his tanned face as though he had suddenly discovered a madman in his party.

"New Zealand," I said, seeking to reassure him of my sanity.

"I'm from Basildon," he said.

Must have spent his formative years watching Antipodean soaps. No doubt about it, I was out of place with these people who were now emerging in ones and twos from the hotel. All were geared up like seasoned trekkers. Already my borrowed boots were beginning to pinch.

Josephine the gambler and her accomplice, Dorothy, came out and sat near me. They each began to scrutinise their fellow walkers with a blatant intensity.

"Seven," said Dorothy.

"Ten," said Josephine. "And they aren't all out yet. There...look! eleven...twelve. Yeah! That's another twenty you owe me."

I was beginning to feel that I would be more in tune with the conversation in a Mongolian yurt. Then the revelation came. The sticks! They were counting the walking sticks. High-tech steel and plastic things with which a number of the ramblers were armed. Down each stick were the letters L E C K I.

My feet survived the borrowed boots but after two weeks I was down two hundred euros to Josephine. It could easily have been more, for she would gamble on the likelihood of any outcome.

"Another week and I bet you'll be in love with me," Josephine challenged.

"How much?" was on my lips, when I saw the startled look Dorothy was giving her friend. Then she laughed with relief, and said; "Just as well we're all going home tomorrow."

I had never been persuaded to have another walking holiday until coming on this one, and again having an expectation of a relaxing, uncomplicated ramble. And now look what I've let myself in for, required to perform as a story teller, the last thing I, or those back at home, would have foreseen.'

There is a short silence, until Jerry reaches for his drink and his listeners realise that there is to be no more. Morris feels let down, his hopes of learning something of Jerry's life unfulfilled. Instead he has had to listen to an amusing story about people met during a holiday several years ago, the rest of the tale alluding to situations which remain obscurely vague. Who persuaded Jerry to take that walking holiday? Mother? Woman friend? Wife? And more importantly, why had Jerry come on this holiday? No hint that it might be because he too was seeking distraction from a broken love affair. Nothing to provide Morris with any opening to release the unvoiced feelings imprisoned in his head.

'What eventually persuaded you to come on another walking holiday?' Morris asks, when they both go to the men's toilet, hoping that Jerry might be in a mood to fill in the biographical blanks of his tale.

'Now Morris,' his friend chides, 'didn't we agree to experience this holiday isolated from the normal context of our lives.'

Jerry had certainly taken care to tell a story that did this, is Morris's indignant thought, with a tale that avoided revealing anything about his life, giving no inkling of what lay behind his decision to take this holiday. They re-join the three women who are discussing the interest Footloose Tales has aroused among some of the others on this holiday.

'Mary has asked me about our group' says Constance. 'I think she would like to join us.'

'A psychologist would have plenty of material for a story,' says Jerry.

'Chaucer didn't have a psychologist—perhaps the Pardoner is closest,' says Morris.

'Not Mary!' insists Jerry, fervently. 'The Pardoner is one of the least attractive of Chaucer's pilgrims: *A voice he had as small has hath a goot...I trow he were a gelding or a mare.* And his practice is despicable even for those times: *And thus with feined flattery and japes, he made the person and the people his apes.* No! not the Pardoner.'

'Let's see how we go before deciding to invite anyone else to join us,' says Diana.

11

Oblivious to the French countryside he is walking through, and barely acknowledging his fellow walkers, Morris's mind is fixed firmly on the task of constructing his Footloose Tale. It has to be an interesting story about events in which he appears in a good light in order to impress Diana with his worthiness. A suitable story is beginning to take shape in his head as his feet bear him steadily on towards the impending narration. It is centred on his intervention in the disintegrated life of a young man, Eddie, who has been brought up in care as had his parents before him. Describing events, such as Eddie's wedding, attended by just Morris and the landlady of the couple's squalid b&b. He as best man, chauffeur and photographer, the landlady matron of honour for Elsa, the pregnant bride. He could include one or two of the lighter moments; Eddie becoming a St John's Ambulance volunteer and using the uniform to get free entry to football matches. The middle of the night phone call from Eddie. He and Elsa, newly housed in a flat, spooked by a ghostly presence in the bedroom, had fled out onto the street. Escorting them back into the flat, where apparently his visit had the effect of exorcising the phantom as no more was heard of it.

There would, too, be an account of the harrowing circumstances of their own baby being taken into care. But should he include details of Elsa's death?

Eager as he is to present his own behaviour in ways that emphasised dedication, skill, and humanity, the difficulty is how to do this without any suggestion of self-promotion, which would surely scupper his chances with the goddess. How far should his tale adhere to the truth? It was an ethical question, but it isn't moral propriety that prevents Morris falling for the temptation of falsehood. It is the certain knowledge that he would be unable to hide his unease about any distortion of the facts when telling the tale.

He doesn't join Jerry for their usual drink before dinner, remaining in his room, fleshing out his story. He sits down to dinner still dwelling on aspects of the story, and when he rises from the table the whole tale is clear in his head, ready to be delivered. He goes with Jerry to take up position in the hotel lounge and finds the most suitable corner of the room already being commandeered by Mary: 'I've managed to find some fellow bridge players,' she tells Jerry, as she is joined by the Merchant. 'My partner, Mark,' she says, '...and our opponents, Thomas and Peter,' indicating the arriving Oxford Cleric and the Shipman.

'Gazumped by the bridge players,' says Jerry, as they manoeuvre chairs at the other side of the room. The three women arrive and Diana deals the cards: Helen gets the lowest card. Deflated and frustrated, Morris has no desire to listen to her story, which is obstructing the telling of his own pent-up tale.

'I've dealt with several oddballs in my life in addition to my husbands,' begins Helen, giving an exaggerated grimace. 'One time when money was tight, I let a room in the rambling Victorian house I occupied. This was before I moved to live in London. My tenant was a young man fresh from university and newly appointed to a job in the county surveyor's department. The room had a shower, and there was a small electric stove for cooking. It seemed an ideal arrangement, he was regular with his rent, played no loud music, in fact most of the time you hardly knew he was in the house. Graham, for that was his name, showed little evidence of the lifestyle expected of a single man of his age. He left for work at the same time each morning and returned at a regular time in the evening. Most of his weekends seemed to be spent in his room watching television, sport mainly, by the sound of it.

I thought the shyness he showed at first would wear off once he got to know me, and he did seem to become less uncomfortable in my presence. He would greet me with the semblance of a smile, but any attempt to engage him in conversation never got very far, he would stand listening to me, yet say little in response. Graham was most at ease with Lisa, my three-old daughter, his face lighting up into a broad smile whenever he saw her. She would smile and chatter away to him, regardless of the fact that he remained silent. In many ways he was the perfect tenant, though I would have preferred him to have been less reticent.

Graham had occupied the room for about three months, during this time he had quickly established his rigid routine, leaving almost to the minute in the morning, and returning at a precise time in the evening. When I noticed he was no longer going from the house at his regular time in the morning, and returning during the day at different times, I naturally assumed he was on holiday. I didn't hear or see him for several days and thought he'd probably gone to visit his parents who lived in the North East. It vexed me that he hadn't bothered to say he would be away.

I was astonished when my probation officer friend, Meg, phoned to tell me that Graham had been arrested for causing criminal damage. He was being held overnight to appear in court next day. What has he done? I wanted to know, finding it difficult to believe what I was hearing. She didn't have any other details but would let me know the situation in the morning after she'd seen him. Graham's door was not locked and I took a look into his room. It was in darkness, but when I opened the curtains I saw that it was much tidier than I had expected, the bed made and no clothes lying about. A neat pile of newspapers was on the floor by the bed, and magazines, mainly physical fitness and athletics, were carefully stacked on a table.

I couldn't settle to anything next day until Meg phoned.

"Graham broke the windows of a doctor's surgery, says it was because the doctor wouldn't give him any tablets," she said.

"Is he a drug addict?" I asked.

Which is what Meg had wanted to know when she contacted the doctor. He had confirmed that Graham was one of his patients, but was not able to divulge the nature of the treatment without the patient's consent, though he did say that the regular medication Graham was on had not been prescribed for drug addiction. The doctor said he would not wish his patient to be punished for breaking the surgery windows.

"Before deciding what to do with him, the magistrates need to know if he has somewhere to live."

"He can return here," I said.

"It sounds like he's got some kind of mental condition," Meg warned me.

"He's been no problem to me," I said.

Graham was given a conditional discharge requiring him to be of good behaviour for twelve months. I was startled by his appearance when he arrived with Meg. His hands were black and there were black streaks on his face. He'd been living rough and sleeping in a coal cellar. His face brightened when he saw Lisa.

"You'd better have a shower," I said. "I'll make you something to eat."

I wasn't surprised when he didn't leave for work the next day, but neither did he go the day after. I didn't see him on either day though could hear him moving about, but the following day no sound came from his room. He was not there when I looked in. He didn't return that night or the next morning. When the doorbell rang I thought it would be him, having forgotten his keys, but I found a young policeman standing on the doorstep. He wanted to know if this was where Graham Benson lived. "He's been breaking windows again."

"Graham's not here—come in and see for yourself," and I showed him the empty room.

"Inform us if he returns," the policeman said, as he left.

Half-an hour later he was back on the doorstep.

"I've to check he's not hiding anywhere on the premises. The sergeant says Benson is a paranoid schizophrenic and could be dangerous."

I showed him round the house and he was on the point of leaving when he asked if there was a cellar. I followed him down the stone steps, sensing an increasing tension in the police officer's nervous flashing of his torch into the darkness. Satisfied no one was lurking in any of the corners, he relaxed.

"Better not let Benson in if he comes back," he said.

I told him that Graham had a key, and the young man advised me to bolt the door when I was alone in the house. Meg also suggested that I should not let Graham into the house. "He's not getting his medication, and could be unpredictable."

"He'll be better off in his room," I told her, 'sleeping rough is not going to help."

In the morning I checked his room but it remained empty.

About midday I had another visit from the young policeman. "Is your name Helen?" excitement in his voice. I told him it was and he said that Benson was holding a pharmacist hostage, threatening to pour acid on him if anyone came near. "There's been no chance to taser him. The Chief's been trying to talk to Benson, but the only word he can get out of him is 'Helen'. The Chief wants to know if you would talk to Benson. There's a woman police officer there," he said, eyeing Lisa.

I didn't hesitate, picturing Graham threatened by a heavy police presence and liable to do anything. The police car took us at speed, its blue light flashing and siren blaring. We were waved through the crowd gathered at the police cordon, people staring when they saw a woman and a toddler get out of the car. It seemed like half the local police force were gathered outside the pharmacy.

"Mrs Harwood?" said a policeman with silver stars on his epaulettes. "Thank you for coming. You don't have to get involved but I'm trying to avoid a nasty incident."

"Graham needs my help," I told him.

Lisa, who was clinging to me, was persuaded to go

with a police woman when she saw the police dog, probably thinking she could stroke the animal. The police moved back from the pharmacy, and I went up to the open door. Graham was in a far corner, almost obscured by the white-coated pharmacist, who was gripped in his arms, an unstoppered bottle of liquid held against the hostage.

I told him that I wanted him to come back to live at my house, but he needed to go to the hospital first. He looked at me as if unsure of what I was saying, so I repeated it, adding that I would go with him to the hospital. He continued to look at me but remained silent. "Lisa is outside," I said, which brought the trace of a smile. He released his grip on the ashen pharmacist, but kept hold of the bottle as he came to the door. Worried by the possibility of a trigger-happy taser cop, I took his hand and led him to the car, Graham clutching the bottle as if it were an amulet. I persuaded him to put it on the ground before getting into the car. Lisa started to wail at being left, and I asked that Meg be brought to look after her.

Graham became an inpatient at the local psychiatric hospital. His parents came to see me during one of their visits to him. They thanked me for helping their son, and said he had talked a lot about being at my house. I visited Graham before he was moved to a hospital nearer his parents' home. He asked about Lisa.

Single Mother Hero was the headline in the local newspaper, with photographs of me and Lisa. And I was interviewed on local TV, the media making the most out of the story. I even received offers of marriage, and my erstwhile husband surfaced to propose that we had another go at being married. The one downside of the whole situation was that I agreed to this doomed proposal.'

Helen sits back, and faces her audience.

'I remember you mentioning this at the time—but I never got the full story,' says Diana.

'Extremely courageous,' Jerry says.

'Good-hearted—honourable,' says Constance.

'Very impressive,' Morris says, feeling that his

Footloose tale will have been diminished by this intrepid account.

12

'Oh, my God!' the piercing cry from Diana snatches Morris's attention from his *blanquette de veau*. She is bent over Helen, whose inert form is face down on the dinner table, spilled wine and water spreading from toppled glasses. He rises to help but Michael is already there, his finger on Helen's pulse. She stirs and Michael raises her up back onto the chair, her eyes fluttering open. The doctor looks into each of her opened eyes, and speaks to Diana, who hurries out of the dining room. She returns holding a small pen-like syringe which Michael takes and injects into Helen's thigh. 'She will be alright,' he announces to the staring diners, who begin to resume their eating, Morris to his cooling veal ragout. Helen is helped from her chair, and, supported by Michael and Diana, walks slowly from the room.

After dinner, and from habit, Morris, Jerry and Constance gather in a corner of the hotel lounge.

'I hope it's nothing serious,' says Constance.

'Lucky that we have a doctor with us,' Morris says.

'And he measures up to Chaucer's physician,' says Jerry, 'who, *knew the cause of every malady, were it of hot or cold, or moist or drye, and where engendered and of what humour. He was a veray parfit practisour.*'

Diana arrives, and flops onto a chair. 'I still feel shocked, but Helen will be okay—Michael is with her.'

She tells them that her friend has an allergy to walnuts, and always carries a shot of epinephrine for emergencies. Helen had not realised that *La Supreme Denoix,* the regional liqueur she was drinking, is made from walnuts.

'Her French must not be very good,' says Jerry.

Diana looks up anxiously when Michael appears.

'Helen is sleeping now,' he informs her. 'I'll check in the morning. I don't anticipate any ill effects from this episode, but if I'm needed I'm in room fifteen.'

Diana looking reassured, thanks him and he leaves.

There are murmurs of assent when Jerry suggests that they could all do with a drink.

Helen is not at breakfast next morning and Diana takes coffee and croissants for her. 'The doctor is there,' she announces on her return. 'Helen seems quite recovered, but will take a taxi to the next hotel.'

'I was all fired up to tell my story,' says Morris.

'A fifty-fifty chance again tonight,' says Jerry, 'you or Constance.'

'I'll just be glad to get the whole thing over.'

'What will we do then in the evenings, our little group when all our tales are done?

'No doubt Diana will think up something,' says Morris.

'A quiz perhaps.'

'God! Not a quiz,' moans Morris. 'I once got thrown out of a pub because of a quiz.'

'I was not aware that a quiz could be sufficient reason for ejection from licensed premises,' proclaims Jerry, in a parody of courtroom discourse.

'There I was having a quiet drink with a companion, not realising it was quiz night until the place became unusually crowded. A drink or two later I was unable to resist calling out answers when only silence followed a question. The quiz people complained to the landlord who told me to desist. I protested that this was a public house in which I had an equal right to express myself. If you don't stop, you're out he said. And that's what happened.'

'The landlord knew where his business lay. You'll have to have some other suggestion if the Manciple's thinking of a quiz.'

The pilgrims usually begin the day's hike with the same companions, any interchanges occurring as they proceed. Today, lacking Helen, Diana attaches herself to Morris and Jerry.

'How are you after the trauma of yesterday?' asks Jerry.

'Missing your friend?' says Morris.

'I offered to remain with her but Michael will be staying.'

'I noticed he wasn't here—his wife walking alone,' Morris says.

'Valerie's his sister. We thought she was his wife—the same surname. Helen says Michael is not married.'

They arrive at that night's hotel, Helen is already there, sitting with the doctor at an outside table, empty wine glasses before them. Diana goes to her friend, who greets her with a broad smile.

'What have we here?' says Jerry. 'I think you can take it that the heat is off. The Wife of Bath is onto a better prospect.'

'What! Have my chances with the Manciple improved?'

'That could be conjectured from my supposition,' says the Man of Law, adopting the inflated tone of courtroom exchanges.

'Here she comes—I'll soon know if anything's changed,' says Morris.

'Helen is fully recovered—she will have dinner and come for tonight's Footloose tale,' Diana says briskly, hardly pausing in her stride. The two men watch her in silence as she disappears into the hotel.

At dinner Michael and his sister are sitting directly opposite Diana and Helen, Valerie looking unsettled by her brother's constant attention across the table. Helen, eyes shining, glows under Michael's sustained gaze: an amused smile plays on Diana's lips. At the end of the meal Morris, Jerry and Constance, secure a corner of the lounge ahead of the bridge players. 'Helen is talking with Michael— she'll be along shortly,' Diana says when she joins them.

Morris waits impatiently, feeling that his turn to tell his tale is never going to arrive. A feeling aggravated when Helen comes and says that Michael has a tale he would like to tell, and would it be alright if he comes along.

'I'm resigned to waiting another two days at most—but

the possibility of a further day...' sighs Constance.

'We'll need to discuss it before making any changes,' Diana says, sharply. 'Perhaps you'll explain that to Michael.'

Helen does not look pleased and goes without a word. The rest wait in silence for her return. But it is Michael who appears and speaks directly to Diana. 'Helen is feeling unwell and has taken a sedative. She asks if tonight's Footloose tale can be postponed until tomorrow.'

'It will be a collective decision—you shall be told of it shortly,' Diana unable to contain her annoyance. 'Where will we find you?'

'I'll wait by the entrance.'

'What does everyone think,' asks Diana, 'do we go ahead without her?'

'I expect Helen needs more time to recover from her collapse,' says Constance.

'I know Helen,' Diana says pointedly.

'What's another day,' says Jerry.

'Let's tell Michael we agree to a postponement, but will definitely go ahead tomorrow,' says Morris.

'Will you go and tell him?' says Diana.

He finds Michael sitting with Thomas. He interrupts their conversation to tell him what has been decided.

'Michael has been telling me of your group, and I wish to present an idea it has given me,' says Thomas.

'Come along now—no one's performing tonight,' Morris tells him.

Thomas returns with him. 'I have been appraised of your splendid activity of holding seminars in the evenings,' he says 'each presented by a different member, and on topics of their choosing.'

'Well it's—' begins Diana.

'—I am fully conversant with the history of this pilgrim route, and have also considerable knowledge of the re-Christianising of the Iberian Peninsula. I would be willing to present either, or both subjects. How would you—'

'—Ours is not an academic exercise; we tell personal

stories, anecdotes, that sort of thing,' Diana cuts in.

Thomas looks deflated, his mouth opening and closing without emitting any sound.

'What you have in mind could be of interest to some of the people on this holiday,' says Constance. 'Why don't you outline your idea at meal times when most people are present?'

'Yes…yes, that I could do,' says Thomas, brightening.

The next evening Morris saw him mounting the hotel stairs followed by three women and a man, evidently on the way to one of their rooms for a seminar. These were older people unlikely to have been influenced in the choice of this holiday by the 'Fancy-Free' come-on in the Footloose promotional literature.

13

Constance intercepts Morris on his way to get a drink before dinner.

'Will you give my apologies to the others—I won't be there to-night. When I knew we would be staying two nights here, and rather than going walking locally, I contacted friends who are camping in these parts, hoping to meet them tomorrow. They insisted I spend tonight with them and are coming to collect me. I expect to be back in time for tomorrow's Footloose Tales.'

'Sure,' he says, and later sees Constance climbing into a camper van.

He explains her absence to the other three when they gather after dinner, and fortified by the certainty of being the only one present yet to tell a tale, he readies himself to deliver his story. But the other three don't want to proceed without Constance. Jerry departs, saying something about taking this chance to catch up with some phone calls.

'Let's all have a night out on the town,' Helen says, eagerly. 'I'll go and get Michael.'

'Good idea,' says Diana, and Morris's pulse quickens.

Half-an-hour later the four of them are walking in the warm evening air, searching for some suitable venue in a town that seems to be closing down for the night. Loud music draws them to a place off the main street.

'Looks scruffy,' says Michael.

'Louche,' says Diana.

'Great,' says Helen, urging Michael forward.

Morris follows closely behind Diana.

It is empty apart from a couple of oldish men drinking at the bar, and peering over the shoulder of the barman who is watching what looks like a porno video. The four intending revellers seat themselves at one of the tables; the barman pulls himself away from the screen of cavorting bodies to attend to his unexpected customers. He stands by their table, this tall young man, silent and expressionless as he waits for them to decide on drinks. He doesn't speak English, and Michael, who prides himself on his French, has difficulty in being understood in that language. 'I think he's Moroccan,' says the doctor. They get their drinks and the barman resumes his vigil at the video. The music continues loud and insistent, chosen apparently for the barman's entertainment, his body moving in time to the beat.

'Let's dance,' Helen says, grabbing Michael's hand, and leading him onto a space by the tables.

Morris looks at Diana and she rises from her chair. Breathless, he takes hold of his goddess and they swirl around the floor. The barman shows his approval by pumping up the music. After a break for more drinks, they dance on, now the only customers but the barman gives no sign of closing. 'I'm sure he's high on something,' says Michael. 'Those dilated pupils.'

For Morris, the warmth of Diana's body, their touching cheeks, brings its own drugged state of ecstasy. The two couples continue to dance until the music ceases, the barman having fallen asleep: the sexual antics persisting on the flickering screen unwatched. Diana takes Morris's arm as they walk back to the hotel. In front of them Helen clasps Michael close to her. Morris's mind, feverish in expectation, is busily anticipating the impending arrangements. His own room can't be their venue tonight as he's sharing with Jerry. Ah! But Helen will be with Michael in his room—Diana will be alone. He quickens his pace and feels no restraint from Diana's looping arm.

In the silent and darkened hotel Helen and Michael make for the stairs and Diana halts. For a brief moment Morris feels the bliss of her lips on his, before she says, 'goodnight,' and turns away, leaving him standing speechless, dumb with disappointment. Anger clouds his eyes as they follow her as she mounts the stairs. He feels deceived, bitter and resentful at the way he has been treated. He goes up to his room, intent on voicing to Jerry an account of the woman's duplicity. But Jerry's rumpled bed is empty.

Morris wakes to find that Jerry has returned to his bed, and is sleeping. Where could he have been in the night? Still dwelling on Diana's dissembling behaviour, the possibility of an assignation comes into his head. Envious of his friend's affable relationship with Diana, the thought of it going further had frequently teased his mind. Has Jerry taken this opportunity to spend the night with her? Morris's fevered brain recalls the two women going to the ladies room before they left the bar—the arrangement made on Diana's mobile. He feigns sleep when Jerry gets up, opens his eyes as his roommate is leaving. 'A good night on the town, then?' says Jerry. Morris is barely able to nod a reply: he could only have learned of their outing from Diana.

He is reluctant to go down for breakfast, not wishing to confront the knowing faces of the three people who are aware of his humiliation. But there is no avoiding them— and he is desperate for some coffee. He meets Valerie on the way. 'Jerry was wondering where you were last night,' she says. Responding to his puzzled look, she tells Morris that she went outside late in the night for a cigarette, where she found Jerry looking to pick up a better signal for his phone. 'I told him my brother said the four of you were going out on the town.'

Morris's spirit lifts on knowing that Jerry was not implicated in last night's fiasco. His mood darkening as he realises he was not spurned for another man, but probably for no man at all. He has, too, yet to face Diana. And there's also Helen, who is likely to have got every detail of the event out of her friend. He passes quickly through the dining room, avoiding eye contact and stopping only to grab some coffee. He sits out on the hotel terrace, where Jerry joins him.

'What did you do on your night out on the town —you and the desired Diana?' his friend enquires.

'Drinking and dancing.'

'Nothing more?

'Nope.'

'Perhaps she's a woman who likes a lot of wooing,' Jerry suggests.

'Maybe, but holidays don't last for ever.'

'Your three fellow revellers were in close conversation at breakfast, Valerie too. Your night out seems to have made Diana easier about Helen's association with Michael...here she is now!'

Morris stiffens as Diana approaches and sits by them. When he summons up the courage to look directly at her, she smiles and asks him how he feels after last night. Is she being wilfully ironic—or simply making a conventional enquiry? How should he respond? He nods his head vaguely, mutters: 'Okay.'

'What do you two think about Michael coming in on Footloose Tales?' she asks.

'Fine by me—I've done my piece,' says Jerry.

'It could mean me having to wait another day to do mine,' Morris complains. 'And what about his sister?'

'Michael says it's not the kind of thing Valerie would be interested in. He would fill one of the empty evenings; the alternative is a second tale from one of us.'

'I don't like that idea,' Jerry says.

'One tale is quite enough for me,' says Morris.

'I'll tell him to join us this evening then.'

'What about Constance?' says Morris.

'I'm sure she will agree—anyway a majority of us are in favour,' says Diana, getting up and going back into the hotel.

At the dinner table that evening a change has taken place in seating preferences, Michael sitting next to Helen, his usual place across the table by his sister now occupied by the Miller. All four seem happy with this new disposition, Valerie, who normally says little to her brother, chatting volubly with the Miller. There is less talk between the Physician and the Wife of Bath, but much is expressed in their absorption of one another's presence, the eyes of each seldom taken off the other: their half-eaten dishes neglected. After dinner, Morris and Jerry established in a quiet space, are joined by Diana, and wait for the rest to arrive. Diana's impatience becoming increasingly apparent by the time Helen appears. 'Michael's putting the finishing touches to his story, in case it's required tonight,' she says.

'I don't think Constance is back—has anybody seen her?' Morris asks, to a shaking of heads.

'It's getting quite late,' says Diana. 'We might have to—'

'—Sorry for the delay,' says Michael, arriving and hurriedly seating himself.

Diana produces the pack of cards and prepares to deal.

' I've waited so long that I don't want to tell my story now without Constance being here,' interrupts Morris. 'I think that the five original members of Footloose Tales should hear all of each other's stories.'

'That doesn't apply to me,' says Michael, 'I'm quite willing to go ahead.'

'Is that agreed?' Diana enquires, and when no one objects she puts the cards away.

14

'I'm calling my story Potluck,' says Michael. 'I've been a keen sailor for most of my life, often accompanied by my sister, though not on this occasion, which is a tale about an experience that occurred a good number of years ago. As a junior doctor I had little money to spare and I was attracted by the remarkably low cost of a flotilla holiday along the Turkish coast. It was described as 'potluck' with no knowing who your fellow crewmembers would turn out to be. Someone at the sailing club had once described sailing in Turkish waters as, "like Greece used to be", and had advised me to go whilst it was still so. I was eager for the experience and in a mood to sail with Captain Bligh if need be.

"OK, you guys. You obviously don't need us," came the voice over the radio. Only five people had been attracted by the fledgling flotilla company's offer, three men on one boat, and my new acquaintance, Wallace, and I on the other. After a couple of hours of keen sailing along the Turkish coast our youthful 'leaders', had been left some way astern. These few words on the radio were music to the ear; we were free to sail how and where we pleased.

The other designated skipper, a bronzed Australian who drank raki neat, agreed that we would stay in radio contact and meet up at various times. I had a feeling that I would need some convivial encounters with him and his crew as there seemed little prospect of much stimulating conversation from my mainly silent shipmate. Wallace had little actual sailing experience but was well versed in the theory and technicalities of his new-found hobby, and had brought several sailing manuals with him. He was keen to learn the practicalities of sailing although his careful and deliberate approach was at times frustrating when the situation called for some urgency. But he bore my impatient demands with a stolid acceptance.

After several days sailing we were looking for a taverna or any place where there was the prospect of a cooling beer, but this thickly wooded section of coast seemed uninhabited. Then it appeared; a table and some empty chairs by the sea edge in a small bay. The anchor was let go in water clear as air and a line from the stern secured ashore, Mediterranean style. The glistening white yacht, afloat on its lucent image, dazzling in the sun's glare.

We headed for the table and the waiting chairs. Above us, nailed to the trunk of the shading tree, was a wooden board on which were two simple drawings; one of a chicken and one of a fish. We sat down and saw up through the trees a dwelling of sorts dug into the hillside. A man emerged from it, stooping under the low doorway; a tall, slender man dressed in the loose clothing of the country people. He came with a wide, welcoming smile, greeting us like brothers. The words he used were unintelligible as were ours to him. There was little need of them to sense that here was a man happy with his abode in the hillside and his collection of chairs gathered beneath a tree.

He took a seat at the wooden table, smiling his pleasure at our presence. He made a drinking gesture and, in response to nods, sped up the hill. Our host returned with bottles of beer and cola which he proudly displayed on the rough table. He would not have a drink himself but sat sharing our enjoyment of his beer. The wine-dark sea of Homer, at this time of day sapphire rather than burgundy, lapped at our feet and shimmered away to the horizon. There was an aroma of pine; a cracking from heated trees; bursts of cicada chorus, and more beer.

I pointed to the fish outline on the tree notice. Our host lost his smile and sadness showed in his eyes. "No fish?" "No feesh," he confirmed, empty hands turned outwards in dismay. We were joined at the table by the family; a girl and a boy, aged around five or six, and their mother whose dark beauty had resisted the rigours of her existence. Come to see the foreigners from the white yacht and to share in the occasion. They sat close alongside the father, arms around one another, mirroring his smile, their eyes curious. The luxury yacht with its tall silvery mast loomed like a threat to such blessedness.

It was time to eat and I indicated the chicken drawing on the wooden menu. The whole family enthusiastically affirmed its availability. They left together, stepping in the dappling sunlight of shading trees, up to their woodland home. Whilst we waited a white sail appeared around the headland, barely moving in the still air. I'd let my fellow skipper know where we had anchored and I waved him into the bay. The family were given to understand there were extra orders for chicken. The Aussie arrived accompanied by one of his crew.

"Bloody Hell!" was his reproachful response to our venue. He said they were on their way further down the coast where there was a real bar and restaurant—a proper place. He was given time to sink a couple of beers before being told that this was where he was eating, the meal already in preparation. Up by the family dwelling smoke was rising from an outdoor oven. From its vicinity came a desperate squawking and figures were darting between trees. Without any warning, Wallace leapt off his chair and rushed up through the trees. We watched in astonishment as he joined in the chase for the condemned fowl and was able to grab the bird. He held it up by the legs in one hand and was in the act of dispatching it by dislocating its neck by the other. He was halted by a gesture of disapproval from its owner at the prospect of such alien slaughter. Wallace handed back the chicken for ritual killing. He returned to his chair with a rare smile on his face.

The chicken finally came to us on four plates with a salad of fresh tomatoes.

"Sure it's tough," I agreed with my Aussie pal, "but it had been quite a sprinter."

We chewed diligently, closely observed by the attentive family. On a scrap of paper the father produced some figures, a ridiculously small sum. We paid our grateful friend the amount he had written and then pressed notes into the hands of the children. There seemed a reluctance to see us go. Leaving in the sleek yacht we waved to the family, sitting yet at the table in the darkening shadow of their tree.

That night we ate at the Australian's intended restaurant. From the sea it was a string of coloured lights along the shore. There was a new jetty and a wooden walkway; a hubbub of voices and Western pop music came from the bar. The owner, smoothly suited, perspiration showing on his forehead, greeted us in excellent English. The menu was extensive. I have no memory of what we ate.'

Murmurs of approval come from his listeners.

'Like an elegy to a departing world,' says Diana.

'It's given me a different view of yachtsmen,' Jerry says.

Morris says nothing, silenced by the quality of yet another tale he will have to follow.

15

A camper van draws up just as the Footloose pilgrims are about to set off on another day's walking. Constance jumps out of the van, waves to the woman driving it away.

'Ruth kept me for another night,' she says to Morris, walking beside him. 'We had a lot to catch up on.'

He tells her of Michael's story.

'Has Valerie also joined the group?'

'According to Michael it's not her kind of thing.'

'I think she's stifled by her dominating brother. I'll have a word with her about joining us. His distraction with Helen will have opened up a space for Valerie to express herself.'

'I guess she's doing that with the Miller.'

'Michael probably hasn't even noticed their friendship.'

The day turns wet and sunless; the sheeted pilgrims tramp along, heads bent against the rain.

'I'll be glad to get out of this and into some dry clothes,' says Morris.

'Not what you expect in France—this sort of weather.' Jerry squelching along by his side.

Damp and hungry the Footloose pilgrims straggle into the village where they are to spend the night. They form a disconsolate group outside the hotel where Dave, looking forlorn, stands in front of its closed door. Facing them, his head uncovered, and seemingly heedless of the rain running down his face, he speaks of a difficulty over his arrangements with the proprietor. He advises everyone to seek shelter in the nearby café whilst he resolves the matter. This is received with cries of protest. 'What's the problem?' several people want to know. 'I'll explain when I've spoken to the proprietor,' says Dave, hammering on the hotel door.

The excluded walkers crowd into the café, grumbling at this delay to their expectations of getting out of wet clothing, taking hot showers and eating a good meal.

Morris and Jerry grab a small table, and are joined by the Miller who manages to squeeze in.

'I knew there was something up,' he says, 'the way Dave's been these last day or two. Money, I expect—it usually is.'

They are still waiting for coffee when Dave comes into the café, a look of desperation on his face.

'There's been a glitz in my financial arrangements,' he says, 'and the proprietor won't budge without an immediate payment.'

'Do we have nowhere to stay tonight?' exclaims Helen.

'We could have whip-round,' declares the Shipman, bringing cries of dissent. 'Well, something has to be done—how much does he want?'

'We've already paid for this holiday—it's not our responsibility,' says the Merchant.

'I'm on a very tight budget,' says Constance.

'We'll see what can be done,' says the Miller, rising from his chair. 'Let's go and have a word with the hotel man.'

Dave looks at him in disbelief, doubt showing on his face as he and the Miller leave the café. An immediate hubbub of conversation breaks out. 'What does he think he can do,' the Knight declares scornfully. 'Sweet foxtrot alpha, I expect.' And there are other voices expressing doubts about any effective outcome from this improbable intervention.

'Perhaps we'll need to find some other accommodation for tonight?' says Morris.

'I expect we'll soon know the outcome,' says Jerry. 'I'm hungry, let's see what's on the menu here.'

Dave comes into the café before there is time to order food, and ignoring the clamour of questions, approaches Jerry: 'Jim needs some legal advice—wonders if you would join us?'

'Okay, if I can be sure of a bite to eat—I'm starving.' He leaves with Dave.

Diana and Helen move to the two vacated places at

Morris's table.

'What's going on?' Helen asks.

'The Man of Law has gone to give advice to the Miller,' says Morris.

'Where is our luggage? I need to get out of these clothes,' says Diana.

'I need a drink,' says Helen.

'Poor Dave,' Diana says, 'everyone seems against him.'

Having decided that there are unlikely to be refreshments forthcoming elsewhere, most of the Footloose contingent are soon occupied in eating and drinking, their eyes lifting to any movement near the café entrance. This vigilance is eventually rewarded by the arrival of Dave, a revived Dave, who holds up his hands to quell the barrage of questions that greet him. 'Come to the hotel when you are ready,' he announces confidently, and departs leaving the many questions unanswered. Morris and the two women finish their meal without delay. 'Get a receipt,' the Manciple advises, 'Footloose should pay for this.'

At the hotel, Morris, reunited with his bag, is in a twin-bedded room, but there is no sign of Jerry. He goes down into the hotel hoping to find him, but only the Merchant, the Shipman and Michael the Physician are there, engaged in heated discussion about the situation.

'Our flights home—will they be honoured?' Mark asks.

'We've got a berth for tonight, but how secure is the rest of the holiday?' says Peter.

'What's going on—do you know?' asks Michael.

'I haven't seen Jerry—I don't know,' replies Morris, and leaves them to their worries.

He is making ready for bed when Jerry comes into the room, and slumps down on his bed. 'I should charge a fee for this,' he says.

'Do you want payment for a situation report?'

'Dave is no longer the sole owner of Footloose, the Miller, or more precisely Wilson Brothers (Europe), now owns half the company. Jim proves to be an astute businessman, and his brother, who I've been on the phone to for what seems like hours, is financially acute, sharp as a scalpel. The Wilsons have built up a chain of profitable garages, and have capital to invest. Footloose was not the kind of investment they would have considered, but the Miller was keen to complete his holiday. He also believes his wife would be interested in becoming involved in this sort of business: "Give her something to do and keep her off my back," was how he expressed it. The amount involved is small beer to the brothers, and will come from a fund they have registered in Jersey. I've been promised a big discount when I want a new car. This is all confidential—if I was working for the practice I wouldn't even be telling you. Dave is to make an announcement in the morning to reassure people about their holiday.'

Breakfast croissants are eaten in an air of expectation as everyone waits for Dave to put in an appearance. He arrives, looking uneasy, and remains standing.

'I apologise to everyone for the inconvenience caused last evening. The temporary difficulty has been resolved, I can promise you that your Footloose holiday will continue as planned.' He sits down at the table and reaches for coffee.

A chorus of questions breaks out. 'What was Jim Wilson's involvement...why was Mr Vroobel needed ...will you be paying for the meal we had to buy at the café?'

'I was there to give some business advice,' says the Miller.

'There were some legal matters requiring clarification,' answers Jerry.

'Footloose will reimburse the cost of the café meals,' Dave replies.

Back in their room Jerry tells Morris that the Miller didn't want it to be known that he had acquired a financial interest in Footloose. He wishes his holiday to continue as before, and believes this would be impossible if he were seen as part-owner of the business.

The mood among the pilgrims is subdued as they begin the day's walk. It improves as blue skies and warm sun help to diffuse the lingering scepticism about the assurances they have been given. The Miller, Morris notices, no longer chats with Dave as was his habit, careful now to avoid any sign of their new connection. Footloose's new shareholder approaches him, an unlit cigarette between his lips.

'I'm out of matches—and Val's lighter's on the blink. Hoped you'd be able to oblige.'

'Sure,' says Morris, lighting the waiting cigarette.

'A smart guy your friend—I expect he's told you what we arranged last night?'

'More or less.'

'Some people have asked me what business advice I gave but I've managed to get away with a lot of meaningless jargon—not difficult after years in the motor trade,' he says, and moves on ahead to where Valerie is waiting.

Morris is joined by Constance. 'I'm glad something was sorted out last night—I couldn't have contributed anything to a rescue fund.'

'Me neither—this holiday's already put me in debt.'

'Surely not—a man who's looking to buy a place in Brighton?'

16

'I'm calling my tale The Cycle of Deprivation. Eddie had spent most of his childhood in care...' Morris silently rehearses the opening lines as he waits for everyone to gather.

'You or Constance—even odds on being chosen,' says Jerry, interrupting Morris's last minute preparation.

'You a betting man?' inquires Morris.

'The occasional flutter,' admits Jerry. 'And I think the odds are about to move against you,' he says, as Valerie appears clutching scribbled sheets of paper in her hand. She comes and sits upright on the edge of a chair, as if preparing to face some painful ordeal. Michael, looking astonished, stares at his sister.

'I didn't think this sort of thing was for you,' he says.

Valerie avoids his gaze.

'Siblings!' Jerry murmurs to Morris, as if this is sufficient explanation of such behaviour.

'You have experience? 'asks Morris, curiosity about his friend's guarded life awakened.

'Indeed,' says Jerry, but nothing more.

'Which Chaucer character can she be?'

'The Canterbury pilgrims were a bit short of women—the Prioress is accompanied by a nun. *Another Nunne with hir hadde she, that was hir chapeleyne and preestes three,*' says Jerry.

Diana deals Valerie a card along with cards for Morris and Constance. Valerie gives Diana a startled look.

'Was it not explained—the evening's tale teller is chosen by card,' says Diana.

'I'm nervous as it is—I can't cope with the added stress of uncertainty,' says Valerie, getting up from her chair.

'Stay and go ahead with your story,' Constance says. 'It's okay with me—and I'm sure Morris will agree.'

'I suppose so,' grumbles Morris, beginning to believe he is never going to be freed from the burden of his undelivered tale.

'Let's hear it, girl,' says Helen.

'Alright, then,' concedes Diana.

'Get me a drink, Michael,' says Valerie, smoothing out the crumpled sheets.

Michael, as if recovering from a trauma, rises slowly from his seat, his eyes fixed on his sister: 'Who else would like a drink?' he asks, after a pause.

He returns with the drinks, and Valerie, after a gulp of red wine, takes a deep breath, and begins.

'I'm calling it Wash-day Dreams,' she says.

'"A cold front will move across the country from the west," says the radiant weatherwoman. Even rain is given glamour. Her braceleted arm gestures towards a line of jagged black triangles which lie menacingly over the British Isles. In the kitchen the washing machine rumbles on. I peer out of the window: grey and drizzly—another dull day. Never get the clothes dry. "Brighter later," said the TV. I gaze out beyond the wet rooftops, become transported through the damp air. In my yacht I hear a different weather forecast. "Malin, Hebrides. West three, veering northwest, increasing five to six, locally seven. Showers. Moderate, becoming good." I listen to the rest of the Shipping Forecast, enrapt by its cadency. "Bailey, Faroes, Fair Isle." Compressed as poetry, the vital lines delivered.

At full spin the washing machine bumps and vibrates, attempts to shake off its piped connections. How much longer, I wonder, will this last? It trembles to a stop, lifeless. The kitchen is silent. A heavy downpour strikes. I sigh.

The depression drifts east towards Scandinavia. From the Polar High clear air pushes a cold wedge under its western edge. In the widening firth there is more light in the air. On the island the mountains unwrap their cover of cloud. In this wind, a little south of west, I hold to a constant course.

The rain ceases as quickly as it began. Is that the sun?

The windowpanes shine; the kitchen glows alive. I unload the washing. Good for years, the gleaming metal of the tub reassures. Outside I twang the plastic line—scatter an artificial shower of raindrops. Wipe it with a cloth and go for the pegs.

Clearing the tip of the island there is open sea to the northwest. The wind veers and the sun breaks through: its warmth falls on the white sail boat. The sea flashes and glitters, spray moistens my face. I suck in the vigour of northern air: clear in my eyes the far islands beckon.

Hanging out bunting, I signal with sheets of brilliant white, shirts of vivid blue, silks of rapturous reds. They billow in the stiffening breeze, purified by sunlit air. I sing their message through pegged teeth. And dream of palm trees; hot sand on my toes.'

Valerie slumps in her chair as if drained of energy.

'Valerie, that was excellent,' says Constance.

'Not strictly biographical—but a good tale,' Diana says.

'I could see myself hanging out that washing,' Helen tells Valerie, whose face has reddened with embarrassment.

Michael stares at his sister with a look of incomprehension.

'The Shipping Forecast is meaningless to me,' Jerry says, 'yet I often find myself listening to it as if it were the liturgy of some hermetic religion.'

'Very imaginative,' says Morris, conscious of a lack of this quality in his story.

17

Valerie and Michael arrive together in spirited conversation, and, in a hotel which has quite limited public space, the enlarged Footloose Tales group is faced with the problem of proceeding in the overcrowded lounge.

'I'd feel uncomfortable telling my story to all and sundry,' Morris says.

'Me too,' says Constance.

'Which of us has the largest bedroom?' Diana asks.

'It's a warm night—what about the terrace?' Morris buoyed by the idea of performing his piece in the open air.

They go out into the soft night, become seated beneath a sky brilliant with stars. Diana deals Constance and Morris each a card, Morris greatly disappointed not to receive the lower one.

'I am a farmer's daughter,' Constance begins, 'brought up on a dairy farm in Cumbria, our land sloping up towards the North Pennines. My father had been born at Whinfell Farm, his parents having moved from North East Scotland. My mother was a local girl. I their only child, a disappointment for they'd hoped for more, and sons to ensure the future of the farm. Gradually, almost unnoticeably, I became the substitute son. At sixteen I left school to work fulltime at the farm, replacing the hired help. My life was the farm, at school I had felt detached from the interests of the other girls, and had no close friends. Boys who attempted to become friendly soon became deterred by my lack of response.

The work I enjoyed most was tending the young stock, the calves and young heifers bred as replacements for the dairy herd. These were housed further up the hill at Thorngyll, a small farm my father took on after the death of the previous tenant, no one now living in the farmhouse.

On a day of bright sunshine I rode the tractor up the sloping field below Thorngyll, the sky seldom so blue and cloud-free. The sun's heat felt through the fabric of my checked shirt, my bared arms hot on the steering wheel. I undid another button. High above swallows were feeding—on a day so perfect I should have been happy. I reached for the throttle, moved the lever and experienced a surge of power as the tractor roared up into Thorngyll's steep yard. I got down and went to the back of the trailer to drop the tailboard, and was withdrawing one of the metal holding pins when the tractor and trailer slipped backwards. I yelped with pain as my hand was trapped against the barn wall. I tried to tug it free, but the pain brought me to my knees. I cried out for help but the only sound came from a distant curlew, its mournful call magnifying the surrounding silence. Sobbing and in despair I must have drifted into unconsciousness.

The face of a young man was looking down at me, his mouth moving in speech. The face went away and I heard the tractor engine start. My hand fell free, and I doubled forward, clutching my crushed fingers. The young man helped me up and pain surged through me, with it came a feeling I had only imagined. I clung onto the man, pushing myself hard against his body, his firm response exciting me further.

On the hay the hurt as he thrust into me was lost in the violence of my desire. When he lifted himself off I lay in the gloom gazing up at the barn roof, still lying there when I heard a vehicle start and drive away. My hand began to throb and I rose from the flattened bed of hay, pulling up my denims with difficulty. Walking unsteadily to the tractor, I climbed onto the seat, and sat for some time unmoving before reaching for the ignition.

"Are you alright?" my mother asked, when I went in the house. She'd noticed that I'd had unusual difficulty manoeuvring the tractor in the narrow Whinfell farmyard.

"Oh! You poor child," she said, seeing my bruised and swollen hand.

My dad came in all annoyed, he'd seen the feed for the Thorngyll young stock still on the trailer.

"What have you been you playing at all this time...?" he

began, before becoming aware of my pale tear-streaked face.

"I'm taking her to the hospital—she's injured her hand," my mother said.

It was dreamlike at A&E, with little sense of being connected with the procedures I was undergoing, my mind transfixed by those indelible minutes in the barn, and this new reality in my life.

"Two broken fingers," my mother said, my dad staring anxiously when he saw me wearing a sling, and my bandaged hand.

"What happened up there at Thorngyll?" he said.

"She doesn't want to talk about it," said my mother. "Shock, I suppose...and she's on painkillers."

Even if I had wanted to speak of the events at Thorngyll, I didn't have the words to describe the experience. For days I was in an abstracted state, my mind preoccupied in trying to understand what I had experienced there, and why I felt so changed. Even now the memory does not come to me with the fluency I would wish.

After a few days, to stem my parents' persistent curiosity, I gave them a few details about the accident. Though I knew from their questioning that they were not completely satisfied by my account, my father wanting to know how long I had been trapped by the trailer; my mother asking how had I finally freed my hand. I told them that it all still seemed hazy, which was not entirely untrue.

My injured hand healed and I was soon able to work as before, but the farm was no longer the complete world it had been, no longer engaging me as it used to. My dad offered to continue tending the young stock so that I didn't have to visit Thorngyll. But I wanted to return to the scene and said I would resume my responsibilities. On my first visit I went into the barn and stood gazing at the place where we had lain. At the spot where a beautiful stranger had entered my life, and who lived on in my dreams. Each time I went up to Thorngyll I was left with a vague feeling of disappointment when no one was there. I began to think that the time in the barn had been another dream: until my periods stopped.

At first I refused to accept the evidence, then tried to hide the fact from my mother, wearing loose clothes, skirts instead of jeans, and remaining in my bedroom as much as possible. As time passed I became increasingly desperate, scared of what my dad would say. I thought of running away, even of killing myself. My behaviour aroused my mother's suspicions and she came to my room one evening.

"Did you meet someone that day at Thorngyll ?" she asked, gently.

I stared at her, then burst into tears. She hugged me to her, I'd never felt so close to my mother. She listened in growing anger, as I sobbed out my story of the man at Thorngyll, convinced that her daughter had been raped. Now she was going to have his child.

"I can't tell my dad," I wailed.

She told me not to worry, she would speak to him. I later learned that he too believed that I had been raped. His desire on revenge against the fiend who had committed this terrible sin against his child was so fierce that my mother believed he would have killed the man. He could not understand why I hadn't said anything at the time, and pressed me for a description of the culprit. He was hardly able to contain his fury when I told him I didn't want to report the matter to the police, and was unwilling to say why. My dreams were not of rape, the fair-haired stranger more like a god than a rapist. This vision was being tarnished by talk of rape—I had to get away.

My mother arranged for me to stay with her younger sister, Grace, who lived with her husband on a smallholding where she kept goats, and made cheese. He did sculptures and made pottery. Auntie Grace was expecting her first child, and the money my parents paid for my stay a welcome addition to an uncertain income. Though I feel sure that she would have taken me in payment or no payment. Over the coming months of our shared expectancy a strong bond developed between us, and I was able to talk to her of my experience that day at Thorngyll. She was the first, and for a long time the only person, with whom I could speak of my sexual worries. Though not even with Grace was I able to speak fully of my darker concerns regarding the incitement of sexual passion.

My son was born in the same week as Grace's daughter. Ben is now working at Whinfell Farm, and with the prospect of a succeeding generation of McKinleys, my dad and I are fully reconciled.'

Constance is silent, a distant look in her eyes. Instinctively Morris rises and kisses her on the cheek. 'So brave…so brave to share this,' he says. She grips his arm; 'Thank you,' she whispers. The profound silence her story has brought on the others becomes broken by expressions of admiration.

'Quite a revelation,' says Jerry, when he and Morris are back in their room. 'I didn't expect the Footloose Tales to become so self-exposing.'

'Neither did I—she's extended the boundary.'

Morris has a strong desire to talk with Constance and during the morning keeps a look-out for a suitable opportunity. Often a solitary figure, today either Diana or Helen, sometimes both, are walking and conversing with her. He evidently not the only one whose interest had been aroused by Constance's story. She is hardly alone for a couple of minutes before he is by her side. She gives him a warm smile.

'It took a lot of courage,' he says.

'I have never been so open before—the memory buried away. It feels as if air and light have been let in. A bit like coming-out—sharing the burden of a shameful secret.'

'I can well understand.'

'You're not gay, are you?'

'No,' he says, surprised by the question. 'But I think we

all have matters that would improve by their telling.'

'I'm sure that's true,' she says, giving him a steady look.

18

'Your waiting will soon be over,' says Jerry at dinner.

'What?' Morris looks up from the table as if unsure where he is.

'The Manciple must be pleased by the success of Footloose Tales,' continues Jerry.

'Yes,' Morris mutters, and pokes at his dish of *ratatouille,* now almost cold. He gets up from his chair and leaves the dining room.

'I expect he's gone to rehearse his story,' Jerry says to Constance, surprised by his friend's abrupt departure.

In the hotel lounge Morris seats himself alongside one of the walls. Silently he rehearses his story, anxious to make a good impression, feeling pressure from the quality of what has gone before. He goes over the sequence of events in his tale about Eddie, but thoughts of Pauline constantly intrude, Eddie becoming indistinct in her shadow. He is still struggling to bring some coherence into his thoughts when the others come from the dining room and seat themselves by him. Morris gets puzzled glances when he remains silent, giving no recognition of their presence. An atmosphere of uneasy expectation is growing when Diana decides to intervene. 'No card needed tonight, Morris,' she says.

He stiffens, sits up, his eyes brighten; a purposeful expression comes to his face.

'The Black Eye,' he announces.

'The black eye changed everything. The injury glaring and emphatic against her pallor, no attempt made to hide the bruising under a cosmetic cover. She wore the blackened eye into the office that Monday morning like a proclamation, a sudden violent announcement of an unsuspected reality in her life. Pauline, the good Catholic wife and mother, who had never given any hint that all was not well in her marriage. For this is how the swollen eye was read, and she did not offer her colleagues any alternative narrative. The black eye shook me, beyond anything I would have felt had it appeared on any of the other women social workers.

In the two years that Pauline had been a colleague my friendship with her had grown. We seemed to have a mutual affinity and took every opportunity of working together. This did not go unnoticed by colleagues, leading to comments about "the dovey duo". I overheard my supervisor one day on the phone telling someone: "I've allocated Yin and Yang for that job," and I did not doubt who he was referring to. Pauline was like a best friend, whose friendship did not compete with my life with Gwen, and in many ways complementary to it.

It was a friendship restricted by circumstances and confined to the working day, but free from the usual obligations, responsibilities and expectations of marriage. She became a trusted confidante, in ways that Greg had been, something I had not expected from a woman. Though, as if by unspoken agreement, we avoided any discussion of our marriages, or sexual matters. Yet there were times when I watched Pauline moving long-legged across the office, or during the close sharing of a car, when I could imagine our friendship blossoming into something more. I resisted such thoughts, my life with Gwen was balanced and stable, and I had an unaccustomed feeling of contentment. And Pauline was embedded in her marriage, ringed round by vows made before God, and whose life was centred on her children. She dressed in a manner that had an almost puritan elegance, her chin-length black hair cut in a plain style. There was never a hint in her behaviour of the suggestiveness exhibited by some of her women colleagues. I knew that any amorous move from me would have destroyed our carefully balanced and sustaining friendship. The black eye changed everything.

Self-contained and distant, Pauline gave the impression of being aloof from the chit-chat and gossip which lubricates life in a workplace. She had no close relationship with any of the women at work, no one with whom she was likely to confide. What should I do? Should I, like the other colleagues, respond to her silence about the blackened eye by avoiding any reference to it in her presence. Though in her absence the eye had become a major topic of office conversation, with much speculation about her private life. Dismayed by some of the less than charitable attitudes being expressed, I was driven to speak of the need to support a colleague in a time of trouble. She seemed so isolated: I could not let her face this alone.

At lunch-time I followed Pauline out to her car.

"I'm sorry," I said.

She stood holding open the driver's door, and looked at me, uncertainty showing in her usually steady gaze. A glint of tears showed in her dark hazel eyes. She beckoned me into the car; I went round to the passenger side and got in.

"Somewhere we can talk," I said.

We were silent as Pauline drove out of the town and headed towards the nearby hills. She was about to turn off the road but checked when she saw a builder's truck parked there. "Beacon for the Millenium," I said. She carried on until pulling off the road into a deserted space overlooking the valley. She got out and stood gazing back at the town. I joined her, looking down at the place in which our lives were being shaped. On this crisp November day it lay mapped out and sharply defined. I could see the office building, and make out the street where my house was; the school where my wife taught.

"I'd known for some time...said nothing for the children's sake. I could keep quiet no longer...faced him with his infidelity." Pauline spoke almost in a whisper, her eyes remaining fixed on the town below.

"And he hit you?" contempt in my voice.

"I was angry, but I never expected Tony to strike me. He's staying at his mother's...Bernadette asking where's daddy. I've tried to keep it from the children, but our row woke everyone, and they ask me about my eye. Mummy stumbled onto the doorknob I tell them, though Patrick's nearly nine now, and I don't think he believes me. I've told no one. Not even my parents."

"What will you do?"

"I don't know," she said, turning towards me.

I had an urge to hold her, kiss the injured eye, but she made an abrupt move back to the car.

"I need time to think," she said, when I got in beside her.

On the journey back my eyes were on Pauline as she drove, competent and assured in her handling of the vehicle. It gave me a feeling of connectedness being driven by her. The pressure of her nearness in the Mini moved me to touch her hand on the steering wheel. It brought a quick glance from her; the briefest of smiles.

"Thanks for listening," she said, when I am dropped off.

"Any time," I said, at once appalled by the crass triteness of my reply.

The colours of the bruised eye were fading, Pauline no longer a hot topic of office gossip. It was in my thoughts that she predominated. There had been an immediate and fundamental shift in our working relationship. The pleasing satisfactions of being in each other's presence, replaced by an unsettling edginess, of uncertainty and undefined expectation. When our eyes met neither of us could hold the gaze, turning away from what we saw there.

On the third day after the black eye, we were together in my car, returning in the afternoon from a court hearing. Suddenly, without prior thought, I swerved into a pub car park, skidded to a halt stalling the engine, and kissed Pauline's open mouth. Her lips pressed onto mine, clinging with the tenacity of limpets. Hot blood coursed through my veins, my body fired by Pauline's passionate response. Indifferent to the discomforts of the car, we became entwined as one enflamed organism in the outpouring of feelings long withheld. The need to breathe uncoupled our lips: arms holding tight.

" Somewhere we can meet," I said, looking beyond the car's misted windows.

"Yes," she said, her eyes on a car parking alongside. "A private place."

We didn't return to the office, Pauline not wishing to face colleagues who would guess the cause of her puffy and reddened mouth. I phoned in, delayed by car trouble I said, which was not quite a lie.'

Morris sinks back in his chair, eyes closed.

'Wow,' says Jerry.

'I could hear more of this,' Valerie says.

Morris opens his eyes, sees Diana staring at him.

'You weren't afraid to tell us,' says Constance.

'Footloose Tales—such a great idea,' says Helen.

'What can we do next?' asks Michael.

'We could meet as usual tomorrow, discus ideas of what might follow,' says Diana.

Morris, bids goodnight to the others, and is asleep almost as soon as his head reaches the pillow.

19

Constance seeks out Morris at the start of next day's section of the pilgrim route. She lodges herself alongside him in so purposeful a manner that Jerry drops behind to leave the two together.

'Where is Pauline now?' she asks.

'In my head,' he says.

'She seems so fresh in your mind—as if it were yesterday.'

'Just a few months ago.'

Constance looks puzzled. 'But the Millenium Beacon?'

'I put that in—I couldn't face telling it as a recent event.'

'I guess there was no happy ending, you being here on your own?'

'I took this holiday in an effort to forget, but the memory of Pauline has lain heavily on me. Speaking about her has given some release.'

'What happened?'

'It's like another tale—not one I'd want to air in public.'

'Tell me.'

'It's likely to pour out like a burst dam.'

'Let it all out,' her eyes steady on his.

'If you're sure.'

He pauses, attempting to establish some coherence in the melange of memories; takes a deep breath. 'The first problem was to find somewhere to make love. I sat in my study bracing myself for this embarrassing quest, which however phrased, meant asking people I knew for the use of their premises in which to commit adultery. My best bet was Geoff, a friend living alone since his separation. I phoned using my mobile—being listened to on a landline extension had brought an untimely end to my first marriage. Hesitantly I explained my request, which was received in silence, then; "I'm sorry Morris, I don't want to be involved. I like Gwen, and count her as a friend. I'll say nothing about this." It was an unexpected response, and a real setback. It also brought to my mind the risk I was taking in revealing my intentions. I felt certain that Geoff would keep his word not to say anything, but who else could I trust?

I phoned Clyde, a man who I'd helped regain the right to have contact with his children. There were rumours about Clyde's present life-style which, if proved true, could curtail this contact. He would know to keep his mouth shut. Clyde was immediately on the defensive when he realised who was on the line. His astonishment apparent when he heard what I was asking of him. "I'd like to help you, Mr Matthews, " he said, "but the woman I'm with now wouldn't have it. I'm in the same boat, looking for somewhere to go with this other woman I've just met." I felt tarnished after this call. What could I do? I knew that Pauline would not find it acceptable for me to come to her home.

Lizzie! The idea was wild—but I was desperate. We'd had a brief fling a few years back, before my time with Gwen, and had remained friends. Her son lived with her but she had no regular man. "You old bastard," Lizzie said, when she heard what I was after. "There's no one in the house during the day—be fine as long as you and your paramour are gone before Jake gets in from school."

"Lizzie, you're an angel," I said.

"Yes—I know."

I sensed Pauline's apprehension as we drove to Lizzie's house. I'd told her that Lizzie was a long-time friend, but had said little more. I found the house key under the garden gnome, and Pauline, visibly uncomfortable, followed me into the house. I led the way up the stairs to the spare bedroom, which Lizzie had asked that I used, and turned on the fan heater she had left, "in case you needed warming up," she'd said, impishly. I started to undress, but Pauline stood unmoving.

"There's only ever been Tony," she said, her voice

tremulous.

"Our bodies will follow our feelings—you have nothing to fear," I said, kissing her and helping her out of her smart jacket. She slipped off her shoes and, with a determined air, continued undressing. She got onto the bed and lay naked, staring up at the ceiling. I lay alongside, placing my arms around her, drawing her close. Within minutes we were consumed with the intensity of our first kissing, untrammelled now by the restrictions of a car interior.

"Beautiful...that was beautiful," she murmured afterwards, her moist body at peace on the borrowed bed. I reached out my hand to fondle her tangled hair.

"I've an appointment— I'm going to be late," she said, sitting up.

Unable to resist this fresh display of her body, I threw my arms around her in an attempt to hold her.

"I have to go," she insisted.

"No appointments next time," I said, and she smiled.'

Morris's eyes blur, and he stops speaking, walking along as if in a trance, bringing concerned glances from Constance.

'You alright?' she asks.

'You don't want to hear more of this—me reliving the experience.'

'Tell it the way it comes to you,' she urges.

'You want me to continue?'

'It will give me leave to describe my break-up with Stephanie.'

'Stephanie!?'

'You sound surprised.'

'I'd thought with having a child and…'

'I've had sex with men since that time in the barn, but it's never been very satisfactory. Only with women have I been able to banish the spectre of erotic pain. Taking up with Steph was like reaching an emotional nirvana.'

'Were you a couple?'

'You shall hear what we were— carry on with your

account.'

'Okay then. We both took a day off for our next visit to Lizzie's house, arriving at midday, me with a bottle of wine, Pauline with cheese and newly baked bread. In arranging this day we had learned something of each other's likes and dislikes; her preference for white wine, and my favourite cheeses. Our conferring over such things bringing us closer—a future taking shape, I thought. We drank some of the wine; use my glasses and leave me a drop, Lizzie had said. But the food lay forgotten in the uncontrollable urgency of desire, both of us starting to rid ourselves of clothing as we mounted the stairs.

Later we ate hungrily in the kitchen, Pauline wrapped in one of Lizzie's blankets.

"Our honeymoon," she said, lifting her wine glass to mine.

"Our honeymoon," I said, drinking.

"What time does her son get in from school?"

"There's time enough," I said, and we headed back up the stairs.

At work the strain of controlling the urge to touch, and the need to suppress expressions of our feelings, brought an awkward tension. I must have carried something of this home with me, Gwen asking why had I become so edgy. I told her I was bit stressed at work. In spite of our efforts, I felt sure that the change in our relationship was unlikely to have gone unnoticed by colleagues. Nothing was said but I sensed the unasked questions and imagined the office gossip. I would have gone crazy if we were unable to have time together, and arranged to use Lizzie's place whenever Pauline and I had matching lunch-breaks. I relished this opportunity for regular sex, but Pauline was not too happy about the short time available.

"I want to lie here longer," she said, pushing herself up off the bed. "There's something lessening about hurried sex."

"I wouldn't like us to give up our lunchtime meetings," I said, already in my shoes.

"Me neither...but there doesn't always have to be sex."

"Of course not," said with more assurance than I felt. Lunchtime sex with Pauline had become high points of the week, my pleasure in no way diminished by being unable to linger.

"My dream is for us to spend the night together— wake in the morning with you next to me," she said.

"A hotel?" I asked, and was answered with a grimace. "I'll see if Lizzie's planning to be away anytime."

"I don't like having to use someone else's home—and it would be wrong to use mine."

"Because of the children?"

"There are several reasons."

I had a sudden picture of Pauline penitent in the confessional and recounting her sinful behaviour with me. I wondered how many 'Hail Marys' I rated.

"I would rent us a flat if I had the money," I said.

"But what will you do?"

"I don't know." The present arrangement suited me well enough and I'd not given much thought to any other.

"I'm separated—will be getting a divorce. You are still a married man."

I was silent, absorbed in the sight of her brushing the silky blackness of her hair, the pale perfection of her face reflected in the mirror. She saw me in the glass gazing at her and turned to me, her eyes ablaze with love. The love, which from our first kiss, had transfused me with an intensity that flowed through my body like new blood. I walked the world a different man, could not envisage life without the love of this woman.

Prepared for the disappointment of no sex when we next visited Lizzie's, my spirits lifted when Pauline showed no hesitation, stripping off with an alacrity that matched my own. I remained lying with her until it was she who made the first move off the bed. I saw no reason why our relationship couldn't continue in this fashion. But my complacency was short-lived, in the car Pauline told me that Tony had got a flat. She had rarely mentioned her husband, and usually only in connection with arrangements for contact with the children. I took this announcement as a pointed reminder of my own unresolved situation. My hopes of an easy solution faded, the most I could do was to delay making any decision in the off-chance that Pauline might feel less strongly about being the sexual partner of a married man. Any prospect of this happening died at our next visit to Lizzie's. My suggestion that we arrange to spend a day's leave there brought a sharp reaction; "No! We have to stop coming here. I'm beginning to feel like a mistress."

I was left uncertain how to proceed, reluctant to take the decisive decision Pauline was pressing on me. But I was overtaken by events. Arriving home that evening I was at once aware of Gwen's unusual attention, eyeing me with a strange, triumphant look. I could see there was something she was eager to tell me, but holding back, savouring the pleasure of anticipating the moment. I had the feeling of the caught mouse waiting for the claws of a contemptuous cat.

"Who do you know on Pickering Avenue?" she said eventually.

"Pickering Avenue?" I stalled.

"Yes—43."

"Lizzie's, of course. You know about Lizzie."

"But not about the tall, dark-haired woman Beryl has seen going in there with you."

This is it, I thought, Beryl, a teacher at Gwen's school, lived on Pickering Avenue and must have been at home one time when he and Pauline had gone to Lizzie's.

"Alright! I went there one lunch time with a colleague," I said, braced for the expected outburst.

"A regular love nest, from what Beryl says," Gwen's manner surprisingly calm, her tone almost matter-of-fact.

I was puzzled. Why was she being so cool about this? I'd thought sparks would fly: her anger might have been easier to handle. This controlled approach touched on my guilt.

"I think we should split—I'm prepared to buy you out," she said, her voice livening.

I was beginning to understand, Gwen must have known of Pauline for some time, and the love affair of my life had become reduced to a business deal.

"How much?" I asked.

"Proportionate to the capital you put in," she quickly replied.

Life, love, marriage, fidelity—the whole complexity of existence narrowed in the next half-hour to a wrangle over money, to a few thousand pounds going one way or the other. The amount settled, it was agreed that I would move out as soon as I'd found somewhere to rent. Gwen seemed well satisfied with the outcome, and her benign attitude had me wondering if she had a replacement standing by.

A week later I was installed in a flat. I'd said nothing to Pauline about these developments, wishing to surprise her with my changed, more acceptable status. She was not at work the following week, having taken leave to be at home during the children's half-term. She phoned me on the Wednesday, said we needed to talk, and suggested meeting somewhere tomorrow when the children would be with their father. She rejected my offer to collect her at the house, and arranged to meet me at a nearby bus stop.

At lunch time I drove away from the office in a joyful mood, Mozart loud on the radio, champagne cool in the boot. Bare-headed, Pauline stood by the bus stop, her hair a black beacon that shone with a purple sheen in the dazzling spring sunlight. She got into the car without a word, her face expressionless, and remained silent until I turned onto the town road.

"I don't want to go into town," tension in her voice.

"We will be private," I assured her.

I swung off the main road and stopped in front of the tall terrace of stone houses.

"Where is this?" Pauline looking bewildered.

"I'll show you."

I unlocked the street door, and she followed me up the

two flights of stairs, where I flung open another door. "Voila!" I announced. "Go in," I urged, Pauline hesitating in the doorway.

"Who's flat is this?"

"Mine...ours," I gushed.

She took a few steps in, then sank onto a chair, and began to weep.

The champagne remained unopened in the fridge, and Pauline sipped instead the tea I had made. My need was for something much stronger than tea, drunken oblivion preferable to the dark void into which I'd been pitched. "For the sake of the children," the wounding words uttered by Pauline to say why our association must end: she and her husband affecting a reconciliation. I barely heard much more of what she had said, deafened by the blood pounding through my head. Tony, a man I would gladly have slaughtered at that moment, already back in the family home, surrounded by his begotten brood.

"But we love each other," I protested wildly, when the room no longer swayed, and speech returned. "I have separated from my wife, got this flat..." I began, the sense of betrayal mounting as I spoke. "Everything you wanted me to do," my bitterness turning into anger. Her reply came in a fresh burst of sobbing. "Hug me," she said, and I could not.

We sat in silence, our eyes avoiding, yet an awareness of her unhappiness grew alongside my self-pitying despair. A mother and her children—no stronger bond! I felt sacrificial. Pauline got up to go, her reddened, tear-filled eyes on me.

"Wait," I said, "I'll take you."

"I want to walk."

I stood up, and we embraced stiffly, a brief touching of cheeks. She pulled away and went out of the flat. The door closed and my tears came.

I woke lying on the bed, still dressed, my head throbbing. I eased myself up and stepped through to the kitchen, stumbling on the empty champagne bottle lying on the floor. I made coffee and stood at the window watching the light fade. Stars had emerged in the night sky when I drew down the blind and moved from the window. I hesitated at the flat door, my impulse to leave checked by not knowing where I could go. I switched on the television and sat for several hours as programmes played out unseen before me. Finally I undressed and got into bed, exhausted by despair.'

Morris takes a long drink from his water-bottle. The pilgrims bunch up at a busy road intersection, and he waits until they are again strung out and his voice can reach only Constance's ears.

'When morning came I was at first uncertain about going into work,' he begins, 'but there were Care Proceedings scheduled that day which required my attendance. I also had a compulsion to see Pauline, in spite of the likelihood that the mere sight of her would be distressing. I arrived at the office, my nerves tensed for the expected encounter. For almost half-an-hour I existed in wrenching suspension before learning that she was on sick leave. It brought a confusion of relief and disappointment, which left me bewildered and unsure. "Unlikely to be back before next Monday," the Office Manager said, showing surprise at me not already knowing.

I wanted to telephone Pauline, make some contact, but knew that it would be pointless. Seated at my desk I opened a file and prepared myself for the Care Proceedings. The mobile buzzed in my jacket, my breathing checked when I heard Pauline's voice. "We need to meet... things to get clear," I heard, her words pronounced with deliberation. "Yes..." was all I could get out. "Yes," again, in agreement to the time and place she suggested. What did it all mean? Was she having second thoughts? I clung to this hope.

Next morning I sat in the café of a large out-of-town supermarket, my coffee untouched. The café was not very busy at this time, its sparsely occupied tables and empty chairs providing an unpromising environment in which to meet. I had arrived early and as I waited my pulse quickened at the thought of seeing Pauline again. And then she was there, about to sit facing me across the table. "Hello," I said, staring intently at her. Seated, she gave me a wan smile. I continued to stare at her drawn face, her dulled eyes, hair that seemed to have lost its shine. I felt a wave of pity for her and the frustration of my helplessness brought tears to my eyes. She declined my offer to get her some tea.

"I'm resigning from my job—working in the same team would be too much," she said, her voice low.

"You must stay—I shall leave."

"I couldn't let you do that."

"I'm going away," I said, a decision newly made.

"Are you sure?"

"Yes," I said, adding, my self-pity resurfacing. "Out of your life."

She sat in silence, looking down at the handbag clutched in her hands on the table. Then, as if a prior resolve had returned, she picked up the bag. "Goodbye Morris," she said, her voice strained, her face averted as she stood up to leave. My eyes followed her as she moved between the tables and out of the café until she became lost among shoppers issuing from the checkouts.'

Morris pauses as they pick their way up a steep and rocky path, Constance silent and thoughtful.

'Well—what do you think?' he asks warily, as the walking becomes easier.

'I have a great deal of sympathy for your wife.'

'For Gwen?'

'She wasn't the cause of the break-up of your marriage and neither was I with Stephanie. And poor Pauline—it seems you would have been content for her to be your mistress.'

It takes Morris several minutes to absorb this unexpected response, resisting an initial impulse to protest at Constance's observations. He was hurt that she thought he wanted Pauline as a mistress. But was she right? The thought troubled him.

'Tell me about Stephanie,' he says

'But first bring me up to the time you became a Footloose pilgrim.'

'There's not much to say. I'd no difficulty in deciding to go away, my roots were not there, and without Pauline nothing to hold me. I had a crazy impulse to go to Australia, reconnect with my friend in Perth. You'll love it here, Greg had said when first there. He spoke of sunshine, swimming, sailing, and the excellent local wine. This had me searching for Margaret River wine, drinking it gave a sense of being connected with Greg. The cards he sent were colourful pictures of the good life to be had in Western Australia. Communication gradually lessened, and I learned little of his personal life: he did mention a partner, but no details.'

'Did you think he was gay?'

'Greg! God no,' Morris says firmly, yet her question disturbs him. 'Anyway, I couldn't turn up there practically penniless and without a job.

With my accrued leave I had only to work one week of the period of notice, and during this time Pauline was still absent on sick leave. The atmosphere in the office was dense with unspoken questions about the sudden turn of events. I rejected any suggestion of a leaving party, and on my final day suffered the embarrassment of being presented with a framed print of a local scene by a well-known artist. I mumbled a brief thanks to an audience that was hoping to hear more about the reasons for my unexpected departure.

So you see, me telling you about looking for a place to buy in Brighton was a load of bullshit.'

'Did you remain with your parents?' Constance asks.

'Yes...my nights disturbed by dreams of Pauline, and her presence with me during the empty days. My mind seethed with thoughts of her, the need to talk of her so pressing that at times I came near to confiding in my mother. To fill the hours I walked the Downs. One day I went along the white cliffs to Beachy Head, it was a fanciful gesture, suicide not seriously on my mind. In fact standing on that terminal cliff-top strengthened my desire for life. The idea of having this holiday probably germinated there when, looking out across to the sea's edge, I decided I needed a complete change of scene, somewhere beyond that horizon. But lying alone on a hot beach would not be the answer: meeting new people in shared activities was what I was looking for.'

'A fellow pilgrim en-route to his own deliverance,' says Constance, bringing a quizzical look from Morris. 'Yes! Me too,' she says, meeting his gaze. 'But I played a different part in a similar story—as you shall hear.'

20

'This is blissful,' sighs Constance, 'the spell it casts over troubling thoughts.'

'Perhaps an unending pilgrimage is the answer,' says Morris.

The Footloose pilgrims are having a lunch stop on a café terrace overlooking a fast-flowing stream. Shaded from the sun's heat, Morris and Constance sit sipping cooling drinks. Jerry joins them. 'I feel refreshed just watching and listening to that water,' he says.

'We could spend the afternoon here—get a taxi to the next place,' says Morris.

'Your idea of a permanent pilgrimage didn't last very long,' says Constance.

Jerry gives them both a questioning look.

Diana arrives, and stands looking down at the river.

'To lie in its water and be taken by the flow,' she says, and sits by Constance.

Dave comes onto the terrace to announce that they will be moving on in fifteen minutes. The two women finish their drinks and leave.

'Diana's lost her role as her friend's marriage arranger. This should be your chance, but you seem to have cosied up with Constance,' says Jerry.

'She gave me the courage to come out with a suppressed memory.'

'Hearing one another's Footloose tales is evidently not enough.'

'She is not clammed up about her past.'

'You and I, Morris, are here with Footloose for different reasons; me to forget and you to remember.'

'The others have started,' says Morris.

They catch up with the rest of the walkers and are joined by Constance, Jerry leaves them, saying he is going to see what Diana is cooking up for ' *notre groupe dans le coin*'.

Constance begins as soon as Jerry has gone. 'I thought Stephanie and I were permanent, owning a house together and having the usual trappings of regular families—except children. We were both keen to bear a child, but agreed it should be Steph as she hadn't already had that experience.'

'How did you decide on the father?'

'The donor was a man Steph had known since their teenage days. Our amateur insemination, the turkey baster method, worked at the first attempt.'

'I don't suppose the recipe's in many cook-books,' says Morris, which gets him a sharp look.

'She gave birth to twin girls. I adored Daphne and Chloe from the day they were born, and felt we were now a complete family. I thought we should formalise our relationship but Steph was reluctant to agree to a Civil Partnership.'

'I thought lesbian couples would jump at the opportunity,' comments Morris.

'She eventually succumbed to my persistence, and agreed. In hindsight the significance of Steph's attitude to a Civil Partnership became apparent. Six months ago she left me, taking the four-year old twins with her. There had been signs of a growing estrangement, but I refused to recognise her attitude as anything more than an aspect of a mother's normal possessiveness. In reality I played an equal part as a parent to the children. Steph's leaving came suddenly and was completely unexpected. The shock shattered the foundation on which I'd built my life: listless and in despair, it felt as if life had drained out of me.

When I finally stirred myself, I received a further blow—Steph and the girls were living with the donor father. I was consumed by intense anger, together with a determination not to lose the twins from my life. Hate replaced the love I'd had for Stephanie, my feelings often unbearable when confronted by stark reminders of Daphne and Chloe's absence. Several times when I'd gone into their silent room I collapsed on one of the bare beds in tears. Desperate to see the girls, I forced myself to phone Steph. Barely able to control my voice, I said I wanted to see the twins. "It would be unsettling for them—the children are happy to be with their mother and father," she said, and cut me off.'

'The Civil Partnership gives you parental responsibility,' says Morris.

'My hopes of an agreement about the children came to nothing, Steph refusing to talk to me. I applied to the County Court for an order granting shared residence. This, or even any contact was opposed, Steph making out that I had not been a proper parent to the children who were now with their real father. Real father! The only fathering he had done was to spurt his semen into a jar. He'd played no part in their lives, Daphne and Chloe never saw him.'

'He might not even be the donor,' says Morris.

'He is—there were DNA tests.'

'What happened?'

'The District Judge ordered the preparation of a report and adjourned the matter to the higher court. My big worry was that Steph would try to turn the twins against me. My anxiety grew as time passed without seeing the children. Eventually the social worker from CAFCAS arranged to see them in my presence. I was shaking as I waited, desperate to see the twins, yet fearful that they had been turned against me. The girls seemed bewildered when they came into the room; the fraction of a second they hesitated felt like an age. Then, "Connie," they both shrieked, and dashed to me to be hugged.'

'That should have been more than enough to convince the social worker,' says Morris.

'She made that clear in the report—yet Steph persisted in her opposition to me having any contact, and continued to contest my application. The final hearing was a month ago. I found it a distressing experience having to listen to her false allegations about my behaviour. But the effort and torment involved sank from my mind when the Judge made an order granting me contact. This is for alternate weekends, and longer periods during holidays when the twins start school.'

'Have the children been with you?'

'A couple of times—Ron, the donor, brings them. He seems OK, sensible and without animosity: someone I can deal with. I'm delighted to have Daphne and Chloe with me even for a short time, and have to resist being-over indulgent.'

'I've some experience of a step-daughter in regular contact with her father— the fierce competition for the child's affection.'

'Gwen has a daughter?'

'Margaret, my first wife.'

'How many times have you been married?'

'Just twice…so far.'

'Are you going to be a serial husband?'

'I don't know what I'm going to be.'

They walk in silence for a while before Constance resumes her account. 'After months of anxiety, with life confined to the one object, I needed a break. This Footloose holiday fits between two contact periods with the twins, a chance to see new places and new faces.'

'A fresh start to life—my feelings too.'

'Both looking for a new woman,' she says, a roguish glint in her eyes.

21

'Our Prioress is a lesbian,' Morris tells Jerry.

'That doesn't surprise me,' says Jerry, searching in his bag for socks. 'So I can end any speculation about you and Constance?'

'Yes…just a platonic relationship.'

'Do you believe in such a thing?'

'No.'

'Can you lend me a pair of socks? I need to wash some.'

'Sure—any colour as long as it's grey.'

At the dinner table Morris and Jerry sit together where a regular seating arrangement has become established; Constance next to Morris, and Diana next to Jerry. Valerie is now seated next to Diana, Helen having replaced her by the side of Michael across the table. Immediately dinner is over, Diana makes an abrupt move from the table. She hurries off without any mention of arranging a Footloose Tales meeting.

'I thought we were going to discuss what might follow our tale-telling,' says Morris.

'Nothing can be decided without the Manciple,' says Jerry.

'I have some cards to write,' says Constance.

Morris watches her as she leaves the dining room.

'It's different knowing she's a lesbian,' he says.

'She's the same woman,' says Jerry.

'Easier to be with—as if she were a male friend. In some ways better than a bloke.'

'Seems to suit you both.'

They go into the lounge, order drinks and seat themselves, expecting Diana to arrive. Morris, whose mobile has been silent this holiday, is startled when he receives a text message. Phone home. Gwen been in touch, he reads. He tells Jerry that he needs to call his father.

Back in his room Morris gets through to his dad, learns

that he had taken a phone call from Gwen about the divorce. Has given his dad the impression that she is having second thoughts about the divorce. He assures his dad that he will speak to her as soon as he gets back. His mother comes on the line, asks him if he is enjoying his holiday. She tells him a woman phoned wanting to contact him. 'Who? Who?' Morris almost shouts at the mobile. 'Didn't give her name—said she knew you at work,' says his mother. Pauline! It must be Pauline. His hand holding the phone shakes as he enters Pauline's number. There is no connection, he tries again and again, in growing desperation, finally accepting that the number is no longer operational. He doesn't have her home number…he could phone her at the office tomorrow. What if the call had come from someone else at the office? The thought cooling his heated brain.

'Not bad news, I hope,' says Jerry, when Morris returns to the hotel lounge.

'I'm not sure,' says Morris, sucking up the last of his cognac.

The Miller, an empty glass in his hand, joins them, he orders another beer and gets them a drink.

'No story-telling tonight?' he asks.

'Our tales have all been told,' says Morris.

'Valerie's told me hers—I didn't know she was a sailor.'

'We've learned surprising things about our Footloose companions,' says Jerry.

'More from some than others,' Morris glancing at his friend.

'We're waiting for Diana to tell us what we shall do next,' says Jerry.

'She's out on the terrace talking to Dave,' the Miller says.

'Perhaps we're going to have a treasure hunt,' jokes Jerry.

Valerie comes into the room looking shaken.

'Anything the matter, Val?' asks the Miller, concerned.

'That John made a lewd suggestion again—when we passed on the stairs.'

'Where is he now?' says the Miller, springing up from his chair.

'Be careful, James, he's a big man.'

The Miller drains his glass, and strides out of the room. A little while later raised voices are heard coming from the outside. There is the clatter of overturning metal chairs. Valerie sits up to listen, her face alive.

'The Miller jousts with the Knight,' says Jerry.

Flushed and dishevelled, the Miller comes back into the hotel. Valerie stands up to greet him, gives him a hug.

'He won't give you any more trouble, luv, or to anyone else for a day or two.'

'Are you okay?' asks Morris.

'The man's just a pumped-up bag of wind,' says the Miller.

'There's blood on your hand,' cries Valerie.

'I don't think it's mine,' he says.

'Come I'll clean it up—on your shirt too.'

'"Today two men fought over me", can go on her postcards,' says Jerry, as he watches them leave together.

'Make a change from the weather,' says Morris.

The Knight does not appear for breakfast, or is present when the pilgrims begin the day's walking. 'My dad's twisted his ankle and getting a car today,' Simon informs the curious. Valerie and the Miller walk together, she gazing frequently at her champion. At the morning break, they both inhale from the same cigarette.

22

'No more Footloose Tales,' says Diana, surprising Morris by choosing to walk with him.

'I guess not,' he says, encouraged by this show of interest, his hopes having plummeted since the heartless end to their night out.

'That woman must have made a deep impression for you to have so vivid a remembrance of her,' says Diana. 'Has there been no one else since?'

'It was all less than a year ago.'

'I had it as nineteen ninety-nine.'

'The Millenium mention is a fabrication—to give the tale distance from the events.'

'I'm beginning to understand why you're here—on the rebound from an affair.'

He bridles at this description, but says nothing: Pauline never just 'an affair'.

'Don't think you're the only one—though not all are as eager as you to begin another,' a teasing smile lighting up her eyes, kindling his hopes.

'How are we to spend our evenings without Footloose Tales?' he ventures.

'There could be something tonight,' she says, returning his gaze with a spicy look that sets his pulse racing.

She drops back to speak to Mary, leaving Morris to his vivid imaginings.

Following dinner, members of the defunct Footloose Tales gather among the more regular Footloose drinkers. The day has been hot and the temperature remains high in this country hotel. Morris can feel perspiration forming on his brow as he stands having a beer with Jerry. Diana, cool and elegant as ever, comes and stands near to him. The complicit look of expectation she gives heats him further. His shirt begins to feel damp on his back, increasing the worry he has of turning up with a sweaty body. Helen is sitting at a table with Michael, her close attention to the doctor distracted, along with that of most females in the room, when Simon makes his stagey entrance. She takes a quick glance across to Morris, and gives him an encouraging smile. Diana moves to speak to her friend, exchanges a few words whilst searching in her handbag. She pulls out and displays card which Morris can see is the seven of spades. Seven! She has indicated to him the number of her room tonight. She replaces the card and accepts a drink from Michael. Morris watches her impatiently, sees a sudden agitation, a quick downing of her drink, and her rapid departure from the room.

He turns to tell Jerry that he'll be leaving, but his friend has gone. Morris hastens from the convivial assembly and climbs the empty stairs with an urgency that spurs his heart beat. He comes to room seven and is about to knock when he hears voices within, one a man's, the other unmistakably Diana. The discovery hits like a blow in the stomach, and he leans helplessly on the door, incapable of movement. The voices fall silent; his imagination takes over: he feels sick. He forces himself from the door, blindly reaches his room, and collapses on the bed. Was that Jerry's voice he heard? Where did he go? The questions burn in his mind. They are in separate rooms and Morris pulls himself off the bed, goes and thumps on Jerry's door. It remains firmly locked. He batters the mute door in a fury. A neighbouring door opens, and Constance, pulling on a silky wrap, looks out.

'Morris! What is the matter?'

The concern in her voice sets off his tears.

'Come on in,' she holds open the door.

He slumps into the one easy chair, Constance sits on the bed.

'What's all this about, Morris?'

She hands him a tissue from a box by the bed, and he wipes his eyes.

'Have you and Jerry fallen out?'

'He's in bed with Diana—he knew I wanted her,' he

stifles a sob.

Constance gets up and gives him a hug.

'Come into my bed,' she says.

He is shocked by this startling suggestion.

'I don't want charity', he protests.

'This is Quaker Charity,' she says, unfastening the buttons on his shirt. 'Pleasing for both donor and recipient.'

Undressed he lies prone on the bed, his face pressed down into the cover. He feels the weight of her body settling by him; her bare arm stretches across his shoulders. Against his will he begins to be aroused, and resists the consuming fire. Her hand moves slowly down along his spine: 'I want to,' she whispers in his ear. He raises his head, and turns to face her.

Their love-making is without the frenzied passion Morris has been seeking, but gives a sense of intimacy not previously experienced, and leaves him with a blissful feeling of contentment as afterwards they lie together.

'I love you,' he tells her.

'No! You are not in love with me.'

'I've never felt like this with a woman.'

'Close, trusting friendship is independent of gender—or of having sex.'

'Like with Greg,' Morris reflects.

'A confidant.'

'A true friend—he wouldn't have betrayed me with Diana.'

'When did you last see him?'

'Not since he went to Australia—about two years after my marriage to Margaret. He was best man at the wedding. I didn't realise what a gap his going would leave.'

'Are you still in touch?'

'An occasional card—that's all.'

'Meeting you is the bonus of my holiday. But I'm not the answer you're looking for—the sexual passion you were hoping to find with Diana.'

'No chance of that now,' regret surfacing in his voice.

'I think Footloose Tales should reconvene for tomorrow's last night,' says Constance, moving off the bed, and putting on her wrap.

'Have you another tale to tell?' Morris reaches for his clothes.

'No! We need to suggest something everyone can take part in. Any ideas?'

Morris is able to think of little else than the coming encounter with Jerry, fearful he will be unable to control himself at the sight of that treacherous man. But an idea does begin to emerge, provoked by the growing sense of irony brought on by the misadventures of his lustful quest.

'Postcards!' he announces. 'A postcard to an imaginary friend about this holiday; written anonymously, placed in a box and pulled out and read randomly.'

'I'll float the idea at breakfast—give people time to prepare their contributions,' she says.

23

Morris is woken by someone shaking his arm, he opens his eyes, closes them again when he sees that it's Jerry.

'How did things go last night?' Jerry asks

Morris stares at the man.

'You dare ask,' he growls angrily, rising up on the bed.

'What do you mean?' Jerry steps back, looking perplexed.

'You were with her,' Morris spits out the words.

'With Diana? Not me.'

'You weren't in your room.'

'I spent the night in Mary's room.'

'Then who…?'

'What did you do?'

'I received solace from the Prioress.'

'It's getting late—you'll need to hurry if you want breakfast,' says Jerry, heading for the door.

Whose voice did he hear in Diana's room? The question torments him as he flings on his clothes. The strutting Knight? Though his importuning of women pilgrims is less in evidence since his clash with the Miller. Not that Morris could envisage Diana going for that man in any circumstance. But there's the son, whose dark handsomeness turns women's heads. He goes through the other possibilities, though there is little to be gained in knowing who the man was, but Morris's curiosity is aroused. He has a masochistic need to know who Diana had preferred to himself.

Breakfast is almost over when he gets to the dining room, only Jerry and Constance are present.

'I've been catching up on events in the night,' Jerry says, grinning. 'From the Prioress here on how she prevented you breaking down my door. And earlier the Wife of Bath told me about her friend the Manciple entertaining our Host in her room.'

'Dave!' Morris had never even considered Dave. He

feels slightly less humiliated by being side-lined by the Host than had it been one of the fellow pilgrims, as if Dave had some entitlement, a kind of *droit du guide*. But the bitter resentment of the way Diana has acted towards him remains undiminished: angry too with himself for the ease with which he had succumbed to her ambiguous behaviour.

'I'd been dreading what might happen when you two met,' says Constance, 'and the news that it was our lusty Host who'd been with Diana filled me with joy.'

'I thought women got turned on by men fighting over them,' says Morris.

'Maybe if you are the woman,' she says.

'I hadn't realised I'd been in danger,' says Jerry

'Not everyone likes your postcard idea,' Constance tells Morris, 'but all are keen for there to be a final Footloose Tales get-together.'

A festive, end-of-term atmosphere prevails among the Footloose pilgrims as they assemble for the final hike on the route to Conques. Morris takes care to avoid coming into contact with Diana, and Constance stays close by him as if she were his chaperone. Jerry is walking with Mary, and Morris resolves to find out more about his friend's unexpected association. His first direct encounter with Diana is at lunchtime. He is with Constance, Jerry, and Mary, at a table in a café garden when Diana arrives. She shows nothing in her manner to suggest that anything untoward had occurred between them. Neither had he seen, and his eyes had been on her much of the morning, any obvious change in her behaviour towards Dave.

'Tonight's our last chance to meet,' she begins, which has Morris turning away, determined not to fall again for any false suggestiveness. 'Your postcard idea could provide a fitting conclusion to our Footloose Tales'

'Challenging,' says Mary, 'to express a definitive view of the holiday in a few lines.'

'You're welcome to join us and have a go,' says Jerry.

'I'll check on my bridge commitments,' she says.

They are on the move again, Morris and Jerry walking together, each absorbed in their own thoughts: Morris trying to come to terms with the debacle of his wooing of Diana. Perhaps she is cold-blooded, an ice-maiden whose character belies her outward form, and he would not have found the hot, passionate experience he was seeking. He dwells on this possibility in an effort to find some acceptable reason for his failure with her. Dave would be able answer this supposition but he could hardly ask him about her performance in the bedroom.

'I can't make sense of Diana,' he says, breaking the silence.

'Perhaps in your eagerness you misread her attitude.'

'I feel like she's been playing with me. But the whistle's blown for time—the game is over.'

'The *mores* of normal life are suspended on holiday,' asserts the Man of Law.

'And not for the better,' Morris says bitterly.

'This postcard wheeze—your idea I believe.'

'I'm already regretting it.'

'Mary immediately saw the difficulties.'

'A bit of a surprise—you and Mary.'

'Mutual affinity,' says Jerry, and Morris knows he is unlikely to get anything more on the subject.

During the afternoon stop, reservations about the postcard scheme are aired. Valerie complains that even written anonymously the identity of the author was likely to be apparent, and wouldn't allow true feelings to be expressed about fellow holidaymakers. Morris too is having second thoughts; the bitter irony that had driven his wish to give uninhibited public expression of feelings, no longer so acute. He readily accepts the decision to drop the postcard idea. Helen remains keen for there to be a final meeting of the group, and this has general agreement. Diana says she will devise a quiz, the women taking on the men. 'Oh Lord!' mutters Morris, under his breath, and Jerry grins.

Constance is with Morris when they move off, Jerry walking ahead with Mary. From what Morris can see his friend is engaged in an intense discussion with Mary. He is only able to pick up the odd word, and would have tried to edge closer if Constance had not been with him. What can Jerry be telling her?

'Has Mary said anything to you about their relationship?' he asks Constance.

'She hasn't—neither have I asked. I think Mary is conditioned by her occupation not to reveal personal details.'

'You're not suggesting Jerry's like a client?'

'Sometimes I feel as if I am—it seems natural for Mary to use her professional skills to help friends.'

Could it be that some psychological problem lay behind Jerry's reason for taking this holiday? It would explain the determination to avoid disclosure of his life. Morris continues to observe Jerry, the occasional word reaching his ears to tantalise his imagination. He hears little to enlighten him about the nature of his friend's conversation with Mary, which they are still engaged in when the pilgrims arrive at Conques. They walk past a large church in the centre of the village, Morris assuming this must be the 'cathedral' that Gunter had spoken of, and where he would have attended mass. Looking up at the tall medieval building Morris's thoughts are with that real and single minded pilgrim, a man who has focussed his life on completing this pilgrimage. Conscious of the lack of any such compelling objective in his own life.

24

For the final Footloose dinner, which he thinks of as the last supper, Morris, alone in a single room, puts on his smarter trousers and wonders how else he can dress to give some recognition of the occasion. The best he is able to contrive as a gesture of formality, is to wear the one tie he has with him, together with a long-sleeved shirt buttoned at the wrist. He arrives down for drinks and finds that most of the Footloose pilgrims, spontaneously it seems, have also made special efforts in their attire; other men with ties, some also wearing jackets. There are women in colourful silks and sparkling earrings: Helen flamboyant and floral in a dress patterned with large pink roses, her eyes prominent with mascara and purple shadow. Diana is elegantly sheathed in emerald green, a silk scarf tied loosely at her queenly neck. Constance's slender body is covered in gauzy white chiffon down to her sandaled feet — 'as befits a Prioress,' she informs him.

The Knight, resurgent after his defeat, has on a blazer bearing some kind of military insignia on the breast pocket, and is wearing a regimental tie. 'I'm surprised he hasn't found a few medals to wear,' says Jerry, who shows no outward sign of treating the occasion as different from any other. There is an atmosphere of restless excitement, conversations louder, voiced with more urgency than usual. 'I'm not sure whether I'm at a wake or a wedding,' says Jerry, above the hubbub.

At the dinner table, Valerie, her usually pale lips graphically reddened, is seated with the Miller who is wearing an expensive looking linen jacket. Further along the table, Simon, suave in a black cashmere polo-neck, is working his magic on the nearby ladies. Constance and Diana take their seats, and Mary, smart in honey-coloured skirt and jacket, sits at the place Jerry has saved for her.

'The occasion demands a bottle of fizz,' he says.

'Some of the regional sparkling wine is as good as

champagne—and much cheaper,' says Mary. She speaks to the waiter, her French sounding confident and fluent. 'We're in luck,' she announces, 'they have some Blanquette de Limoux, a wine I can personally recommend.'

Replete with food and wine, the Footloose Tales group eventually gather after the prolonged meal, but show little enthusiasm for anything more testing than gossipy conversation. Even Diana seems to have lost the will to pursue her intention of holding a quiz. Valerie takes herself off to re-join the waiting Miller.

'That Simon—thinks he's a gigolo,' says Helen, slurring her words.

'The father—,' Mary begins.

'Our *parfit gentil knight,*' Jerry interjects.

'—behaves like a conman.'

'He's tried to sell me shares in a company he owns,' says Constance.

'A fine pair of pilgrims, those two,' says Michael.

He and Helen leave, then Constance and Mary bid everyone 'goodnight', and shortly afterwards Diana goes, watched by Morris and Jerry. 'Footloose Tales,' says Jerry, 'out with a whimper, not with a bang.' Morris, regards his empty glass, thinks of his empty bed.

He is on the verge of sleep when a text from his mother jolts him fully awake. The woman from work has phoned again, no name but left a phone number. Morris doesn't recognise the number, it's not the office and he doesn't remember Pauline's home number, never having used it, but it's the local code and could only be hers. His thoughts race over the possible reasons for this contact, returning each time to her wishing to resume their relationship. What had brought this about? Had the 'for the sake of the children' reconciliation fallen apart?

There came into his mind something that would never have arisen just a short time ago, desperate then to clutch at any chance of renewing their relationship. Could he bear to repeat the trauma of the break-up? Yet there would be this risk; Pauline, a mother who would always put the interests of her children first. It shook him that he was thinking in this way, disloyal to the memory of their love. Sleep is a long time in coming, his mind mulling over the possibility of a change in Pauline's attitude. Had he himself changed? Can rapture be recaptured?

25

Morris wakes with a headache, still troubled by the thoughts that had kept him awake. Opening the curtains, he sees that the coach for the airport is already here. He needs to talk to Constance about this approach from Pauline—will there be time? He throws his belongings into the travelling bag and goes down to grab some breakfast. There is an air of transience in the dining room, the few Footloose pilgrims still present seem distracted, their thoughts elsewhere, as if the life that re-awaits them is already beginning to intrude.

Jerry appears carrying his case. 'I checked your room—thought you might miss the bus.'

'Have you seen Constance?'

'She was here earlier having *petit déjeuner*. Dave says we have to leave in five minutes.'

Morris gulps down the rest of his coffee, picks up his bag, and follows Jerry out of the hotel. They dump their bags in the luggage hold and Dave follows them onto the coach: 'That's everybody,' he says. Morris looks for Constance but she is sitting with Mary: he must talk with her before she is gone forever. He sees that Michael is sitting with Helen, and the Miller with Valerie. The empty seat by Diana acts on Morris like an invitation, but he resists the temptation, and sits with Jerry. The coach moves off, and Dave, having attended to the immediate wants of his Footloose flock, settles himself by Diana.

Emerging from the irksome process of airport security, Morris goes in search of Constance. She is with several of the others getting drinks and snacks.

'Is there somewhere we can talk?' he says, when she asks if there's anything she can get him. She nods and leads the way to a less crowded part of Departures.

'Pauline has been trying to get in touch,' he blurts out as soon as they are seated. He tells her of the message from his mother.

'Are you sure it's Pauline?'

'There's no one else it could be.'

'Your wife?'

'That's the other thing, Gwen's phoned my parents—given them the impression that she's now undecided about the divorce. I don't know what to do.'

'I'm surprised you're even considering what you should do.'

'I don't want to go through that hurt again.'

'I thought you'd risk anything to be with Pauline?'

'What keeps coming into my mind is the saying, *no man ever steps in the same river twice—*'

'*—for it's not the same river and he's not the same man,*' continues Constance, 'though I doubt whether Heraclitus would recognise this rendering, still less the feminist version. Ruth and I are going to have another go at living together, hoping that we are no longer the same women who failed the first time. The message I take from Heraclitus is that if you do go back to a previous situation, don't expect it to be the same. It might even be better—perhaps your marriage?'

'Gwen is dedicated to her profession—the education of children with special needs.'

'Were you jealous that much of her attention was going elsewhere?'

'It was her strong sense of purpose I resented. She said she had discovered her vocation, and I was pierced with envy.' Morris becomes silent, his brows contorted by the strain of his thoughts.

'I've led an aimless, headlong life.'

'Surely there is purpose in your work?'

'Dealing with other people's lives and problems? —a distraction from my own. Where am I going…how am I to fill the emptiness ahead? In the past I've sought to lose myself in sexual adventures—my purpose in coming on this holiday. And suppose I had made it with Diana, enjoyed a few days of sexual bliss, what then? It would not be the answer—it never has been. There has to be something else—and you have opened my eyes to that possibility'

'That's our boarding call,' says Constance, getting up from her seat.

On the plane the cohort of Footloose pilgrims, who have populated Morris's world for the last two weeks, are dispersed among the other passengers, their group identity fragmenting. An unknown man is on the aisle seat of the row where he and Jerry are sitting. Morris becomes preoccupied by thoughts of the uncertainties he is flying back to, and Jerry too is silent, gazing out of the window at the limitless sky. If Gwen no longer wants to go ahead with the divorce, what has changed her mind? And what will she be expecting of him? As for Pauline—everything is based on supposition, even the identity of the caller not absolutely certain. Though he does not doubt that it would be Pauline who will answer when he dials that number, or that she wishes to resume their relationship. He tries to imagine being part of her household, and taking on the role of step-father to the children for whom he had previously been forsaken. He is no clearer in his mind when the plane begins to descend. 'Terra firma,' says Jerry, fastening his seat-belt.

Constance is already at baggage reclaim when Morris gets there, and he stands by her as the carousel begins to turn. 'It's like a big roulette wheel where everyone expects to get a prize,' she says. Luggage is now circulating, and Morris observes former Footloose pilgrims as they collect their bags, randomly distributed by the determining wheel. Most leave as soon as they retrieve their luggage. He grabs his own bag. 'I'll wait,' he tells Constance, who is still on the look-out for hers. Jerry, nearby, pulls his bag off the carousel, and steps closer to Morris.

'I've greatly enjoyed knowing you,' he says, 'but don't expect a Christmas card.' He puts a hand on Morris's shoulder, who responds with a clumsy one-armed hug. 'Goodbye,' says Morris, barely able to contain the sadness he feels as he watches his transient friend walk away.

He gets a brief wave from Helen as she and Diana leave together. Michael and Valerie have already gone, brother and sister with one another. Jim presses a business card into Morris's hand as he passes by: 'Contact me when you want to change your car,' he says. Constance's bag finally appears on the circuit, she and Morris almost the last of the pilgrims to leave.

'It's like a reversal to the start of the holiday,' she says, 'people leaving as they came, alone or with the same person.'

'Holiday romances,' says Morris.

'Our friendship will be more than that,' she says.

'Promise you won't go to Australia.'

'I won't be far away—I need you too.'

Together they walk to the station, for different destinations.